JOHN LUDDEN

Intro:

Blackpool today: The old man sits by the window in a one room flat facing the promenade and only a hundred yards from the town's funfair. His ninety years and plus have been a painful existence. Forced to hide his true identity for over seventy years, the old man speaks little and views life like an affliction.

A curse that can only be lifted when death comes calling to release him from this prison cell without walls called living.

So many times the old man has thought about taking his own life. One moment of courage would be all it takes to end the nightmares and make the memories fade away to black. Now as reality beckons and the days grow infinitely harder.

The shortness of breath and the stomach pains cripple. The blood, so much blood. The fear grows daily for he knows there has to be payback.

A day of reckoning is dawning where the old man will be held to task for his heinous crimes. The sins of the father and his own dreadful acts must be paid for in this life or the next.

He watches as the never-ending carnival that is Blackpool parties on outside his window. It was the same back then. The beer and the laughter, the girls forever willing, the men even more. It was here he carved his own small notch in history. One unwritten.

Until now.

So many times before and after the old man has looked in the mirror and the face that stared back was of another.
One that once upon a time in Blackpool,
everybody knew the name of.

MANY YEARS AGO...

MOLLY

September 1940: It is the last encore and in Blackpool's Tower Ballroom, hundreds of dance couples take to the floor at the opening chords of Glenn Miller's *In the Mood*. A packed auditorium heaves with Army, Navy and RAF uniforms, plus civilians. The women, beautiful, plain, shapely, thin and fat. All plucked off the tables and sidelines to participate. None are left standing.
It is orgiastic.
Dunkirk was two months previous. England holds its breath for the Germans are expected to invade at any moment. A feeling of live for the moment because you're most likely to be dead tomorrow is in the air.
People's inhibitions have disappeared. Eat, dance, drink and make love for the hooves of the Nazi war machine are closing in. They are set to take these things away.
None more have grasped the mood than pretty local girls, eighteen year olds, blonde Molly Gardiner, and long dark-haired, Amy Roberts. They are enjoying being hurled around the dance floor by two equally young soldiers. Mancunian, nineteen year old, Eddie Potter and Scouser, twenty year old, Billy Cardus.
An announcer takes to the mic.

'Ladies and gentlemen. Thank you for a wonderful evening. Please before you make your way out, be upstanding for God Save the Queen.'

Another man comes on the mic and in Polish repeats the request.

Respectfully the hundreds of Poles present stand equally still.

At the finish there are huge cheers. A spontaneous rendition of Poland's anthem now breaks out amongst them. At the finish it is roundly applauded by all. Finally in a raucous atmosphere, people begin to make their way in an orderly, if exuberant manner out of the Tower ball room.

Along a darkened Blackpool prom. The illuminations taken down and stored away in a bus depot for hopes of a better day. Molly is linking Eddie whilst Amy and Billy do similar.

Molly turns to Eddie. 'Who fancies fish and chips then?'

He smiles. 'I can think of something else I fancy more Molly love!'

Eddie tries to kiss her on the cheek, but she pulls away. 'Behave yourself soldier boy. Me and my friend are not that kind. Are we Amy?'

Molly turns around and sees Amy and Billy kissing passionately.

Eddie is insistent. 'C'mon Molly girl. Just a peck on the cheek.'

'Well I'm not that kind of girl.'

Amy pulls away from Billy on hearing this.

She's angry. 'What's that supposed to mean Molly?'

'Yeah what's that supposed to mean Molly? 'Laughs a drunken Billy.

Molly is upset. 'I want to go home.'

'Well I don't' replies an indignant Amy.

'I'll come with you Moll' adds Eddie

Angry and upset Molly snaps. 'Stay away from me. I'm going home on my own.'

A crying Molly runs off down the prom into the blackness.

Amy panics at seeing her friend disappear. 'Molly please come back...Molly.'

Eddie also. 'Molly, come on girl. I'm sorry.'

Molly doesn't reply.

The night swallows her up.

The next morning in a backstreet hotel bedroom, twenty six year old Harry Carter. Handsome, lean with dark hair and sparkling blue eyes awakes.

A naked Carter sits up on the edge of a bed.

He lights a cigarette and looks out a window with a view of the prom. There is someone else in the bed, but they are still asleep.

A seagull lands on the ledge and is staring at Carter. He stares back.

'What are you looking at you crazy bird?'

The seagull continues to stare.

A ruffle of the sheets and the other person awakes. It is twenty three year old Army Corporal, George Rafferty. Northern Irish. Boyish looks, tall, well built with blond hair.

Rafferty smiles. 'Good morning. Can I have one of those?'

He points to Carter's cigarettes who throws him the packet. Rafferty sits and lights up.

'I have to go to work' says Carter. 'I'll leave first, you follow. Watch nobody sees you leave the room.'
Rafferty looks admiringly at Carter. 'So how come you're not in the forces? What do you do for a living then?'
Carter is busy getting dressed. 'I'm a copper.'
Rafferty starts to laugh. 'Christ I've just slept with a copper!'
'Hey' snaps Carter. 'Anyone catches us we're both in deep trouble.'
'Calm down Harry. Don't you know it's the end of the world? The Germans will be here in a month. I was lucky enough to survive Dunkirk. And now we've orders to fight to the death when they arrive here.
So Mr Policeman, I'm making the most of the time I've left.'
Carter is changed and ready to go.
He puts his trilby on. Placing it low over his eyes.
'Remember what I said, be careful when leaving.'
He turns to go, only for Rafferty to shout after him
'Hey Mr Policeman, will I see you again?'
'Only if you break the law' replies Carter.
Rafferty grins wide. 'What do you call last night then?'
Carter can't help but smile. 'So long soldier boy.'

Later that morning Detective Harry Carter is walking over a huge deserted beach towards the pier. Already under it are a haggle of policemen, both uniformed and plain clothed. Chief Detective, fifty four year old Sidney Appleton. Haggard features, a wizened and experienced copper approaches Carter.
'Here he is Blackpool's finest. Where the bloody hell have you been? I knocked at your house first thing this morning, but no answer?'

Carter smiles. 'I went to the pictures last night. Stayed at a lady friends. One of the usherettes. I got lucky.'

Appleton shakes his head. 'You never stop you dirty sod. C'mon we've got work to do.'

Carter and Appleton stand over a badly cut up woman's body. Her face slashed to ribbons.

'What did the bastard use?' Asks Carter

'A razor. Never seen anything like this. Look, he's sliced a fuckin' Swastika onto the poor cow's forehead.'

Carter crouches down over the body. 'Jesus Christ.'

'Appleton reads from a piece of paper. 'The girl's name is Molly Gardiner. Eighteen years old. A local kid.'

'Who found her?'

'An air warden. Jack Hardy. He's pretty shook up.'

Appleton points towards an ashen faced, sixty year old Hardy, who is stood nearby being questioned by a constable.

Carter goes across. 'You okay Jack? I'm Detective Carter.

Hardy appears close to tears. He stares over towards Molly's body.

'I'm no shrinking violet Mr Carter. I was in the trenches. I saw some terrible things, but this? What that bastard has done to that girl? It's just evil, pure evil.'

'We'll get him Jack. You say you found the body just after six this morning? You've been around here all evening. Did you see anyone or anything that might be classed as suspicious?'

'No nothing. Just the usual. Drunken soldiers trying to get back to barracks. Boisterous, but nothing more. You know what it's like Mr Carter. Poles, our own lads. All drinking too much, but we know what's round the corner for them. Most are nothing but kids.

But this?'

Hardy points to Molly's body. 'This is beyond evil.'

Carter pats Hardy on the shoulder.

'Thanks Jack. Now go and get a cup of tea with the constable here. We'll get a full statement later.'

Hardy goes to walk off with the constable, only to suddenly turn around and face Carter. 'You don't think it's the bloody Germans do you? I mean the Swastika thing. Maybe they are just trying to put the fear of God into us?'

Carter smiles. 'No it's not Adolf and his cronies. It'll be another maniac, but we'll get him Jack. I promise you. Now go on.'

As a shaken Hardy is lead away with the Constable, a voice suddenly makes Carter jump.

It is the Blackpool Gazette's chief hack, forty five year old, Len Hammond. A lived in face, short in height with a permanent cigarette in the corner of his mouth. 'Fuckin' ell Harry, what have we got here?'

Hammond stands with notebook in hand.

'Len I need a favour mate.'

Carter puts an arm around Hammond's shoulders as they head back towards the pier. 'What kind of favour?'

'We've got to keep a lid on this case. Blackpool can't afford the panic. Just give us a couple of days to catch whoever did it and then we'll give you the full scoop on the entire story. I promise. You get the glory. People around here have enough to worry about. We really need your help on this old pal.'

'Okay then' smiles Hammond. 'Seeing as it's you. A couple of days it is.'

They arrive under the pier. Hammond catches sight of the body close up.

'Oh my good God!'

He rushes off and is violently sick on the sand.

Carter returns to the body. He stands alongside Appleton.

'So where do we start?' Asks Carter

Appleton appears mesmerised by Molly's corpse. 'Far be it from me to denigrate our brave allies in this almighty struggle to come, but first port of call for me and you my lad is a little chat with our Polish guests. Come on.'

The policemen walk past a still vomiting Hammond on his knees.

'Make sure you bury that Len' shouts Appleton. 'We don't want the fuckin' donkeys stepping in it.'

Carter tries hard not to laugh.

In a backstreet bedsit, Twenty-seven year old Freddie May. Beady, snake-like eyes. Small of height with black hair and a tiny dribble of a moustache is in the Bath tub. He dips his head under the water then surfaces. May breaks into a huge grin. He looks at the red streaks still stuck under his finger nails. Molly Gardiner's blood...

POLISH DESCENT

Lansdowne Hotel: Polish Headquarters: Forty-nine year old General Stanislaw Sosabowski. Tall, moustached, charismatic leader of the free Polish forces is not a man to mince his word or suffer fools. Loved and respected by all who serve with him, not one soldier under Sosabowski's command would not lay down their life for the General. There are over ten thousand Polish military and air force personnel billeted around Blackpool. All desperate for another crack at the Germans.

Forced to flee their homeland, Sosabowski has vowed one day the Poles will return home as free men. Until that time they have pledged to fight alongside the British now hovering on the brink of disaster and a Nazi invasion.

A feeling sadly all too familiar to the Poles.

Sosabowski is sat at his desk in the front of the hotel when there's a knock on the door and Appleton and Carter enter.

Appleton smiles. 'General Sosabowski. We did ring ahead. Thank you for seeing us so swiftly. I'm Chief Inspector Appleton. This is my colleague Detective Carter.'

A grim faced Sosabowski motions for the two men to sit down.

'Please gentlemen. This is terrible news. What can I do for you?'

Appleton continues. 'General, we don't kid ourselves. Away from all the fun of the prom this town has always been a den of ill repute. I think it's something in the sea air. We attract rascals, villains, vagabonds and thieves. Manchester's and Liverpool's finest. But we've never seen. I've never seen in all my twenty years on the Blackpool beat. Anything like what I witnessed under that pier this morning.'

Sosabowski does not look impressed. 'So if I'm reading you rightly Mr Appleton, you and your friend here believe the culprit of this butchery is of Polish descent. Am I right?'

'Not necessarily sir,' replies Carter. 'We are just.'

Appleton interrupts. 'I'm just doing the maths General. A logical first step in our enquiries.'

'You believe no Englishman is capable of this vile act?' Replies Sosabowski.

'Like I said. All lines of enquiries. There will be others we shall follow.'

Sosabowski is clearly irked. 'Let me tell you something Chief Inspector Appleton. When the enemy comes to these shores you will be grateful for those you consider worthy of your first line of enquiry. We Poles have fought the Nazis on our own soil. We have seen the beast up close. And now my men are willing to fight and die for this country that is not their own. You may ask why?'

Both policemen decide best just to let him carry on.

'Well we are a proud and honourable people. We give our lives for our allies and expect little in return. Maybe just respect. A little thing but one you gentlemen may wish to consider.'

Appleton attempts to calm waters. 'I didn't mean any disrespect General Sosabowski. I'm just doing my job.'

Sosabowski nods, as if in agreement. But he is clearly still seething.

'I believe you are. I will assign one of my officers to act as liaison. Now if that is all, I have a lot of work to do. There is an invasion to plan for.'

Appleton and Carter stand to leave. 'Thank you for your time sir,' says Appleton, going to shake Sosabowski's hand.

But he doesn't accept it. The General simply glares angrily at them.

'You can see yourself out. My man will be in touch.'

Looking duly admonished Appleton and Carter put on their trilbies and leave the office.

Once outside and on the pavement Carter can't help himself.

'Well that went fuckin' well. I think you've just started a war with Poland.'

A stone faced Appleton stares at a smiling Carter. He goes to playfully knock his hat off. 'C'mon you, we've got work to do.'

'Where are we going?' Asks Carter.

'Paddy Owen's.'

'Are you sure boss? Last time I looked Paddy is one of the biggest villains in the north of England. The king of the black market and God knows what else?'

'Absolutely young man. And what else? That's my point. Nothing happens in this town without Paddy knowing about it. We need to nail this mad bastard and quick. Paddy can help us do that. It's time to kick a few arses Harry lad.'

BABYLON BY THE SEA

Empire Ballroom: Mancunian born, forty seven years old Patrick Owen. Tall, lean. Quiffed, slick back oiled hair. A dander. A gentleman gangster. A man about town, Smart and classy.

Blackpool's top rogue.

Owen is sat in the ballroom watching his scantily clad showgirls being put through their moves up on the stage. Appleton and Carter enter and walk towards him. They stop facing Owen.

'Hello Paddy' says Appleton.

Owen smiles. 'Hello Sidney, Harry. To what do I owe this honour?'

The loud music from the stage makes it hard to hear. Appleton continues but is forced to shout. 'Can we speak outside?'

Owen nods. He points to the exit and they leave.

In the bar Owen serves three large whiskies. He looks over at his two guests and passes them their glasses.

'Well gents what can I do for you?'

'I suppose you've heard about the young girl found murdered under the pier?' 'Blackpool is a small town. Of course, it's a lousy thing. But what has that to do with me?'

'We need your help' replies Appleton. 'You know how it is, people are already on edge with the Germans on the way. If this was to happen again?'

Owen takes a drink. 'Is it true about the Swastika carved into the kid's head?'

Appleton nods.

Shaking his head Owen looks disgusted. 'Jesus Christ. Okay then I'll get the boys rounded up and asking questions. We might need to break a few thumbs, blacken a few eyes. Is that alright with you?'

'Desperate times Patrick,' replies Appleton. 'Whatever it takes.'

''I'll make calls myself as well. I tend to find a personal appearance can loosen tongues. Must be my sparkling personality.'

'Or maybe a knuckle duster?' Adds a smiling Carter.

'Thanks Paddy' says Appleton. 'I want this piece of work behind bars and swinging before God forbid he gets the urge to do it again. My rare experience with freaks like this is once they get a taste of blood they don't stop.'

Owen refills all three glasses. He hands one each to Carter and Appleton.

'I know you're on duty but drink up. Dark skies are drawing in boys. These are the last days of Rome. Blackpool is Babylon by the sea. There are no inhibitions anymore. Every deviant, drug fiend and sexual freak is being catered for between the north and south pier.

We have soldiers enjoying a last blow out.

Thousands of Poles drinking themselves into oblivion and lonely housewives and young girls more than willing to spread their legs for king and fuckin'country.

Normality is over for the thought of what's coming is making people put on their best clobber, drink themselves silly and party like it's the end of the world. Welcome to fuckin' Blackpool.'

Owen lights up a cigarette on a solid gold lighter.

'All that apart, I promise I'll do my best to help you find this creep.'

Carter drinks his whiskey in one go. 'Thanks Paddy. What are your plans for when Adolf turns up? I can't see you going quietly into the night.'

Owen smiles. 'Just the one. I've saved myself a couple of rare bottles of fine Scotch. I'm going to get drunk as a skunk, fill this place here with Nazis. Sing God save the King, and then I'm going to blow it sky high with a box of TNT dynamite, I'm keeping in the cellar for special occasions.'

Appleton appears a little taken aback, but then smiles. 'Special occasions?

I never heard that.'

In the kitchen of the Grand Metropole hotel, Freddie May is drying a huge pile of plates and dishes. He drops one and it smashes.

May's superior, Thirty four year old Albert Longdon. A bully, fat, balding and red faced explodes in anger at May. 'You clumsy idiot. That's the third time today. Since you've been working here, you've done more damage than the fuckin' Luftwaffe ever could to this kitchen. I've had it with you. You're fired. Get out.'

May stares at Longdon. A look of sheer hatred. It appears to unnerve him.

'Just get your stuff and go!'

Still May stares. Around him fellow workers watch transfixed. Finally he takes off his apron and throws it at Longdon.

May walks slowly out of the kitchen. Nobody says a word. There is something about the quiet dishwater that makes all present uneasy. And a little scared.

It is early evening as May heads across the main road and onto the now, near empty beach. The sea is far out and he sits down.

A blond woman, a prostitute. Forty three year old Cork born, Mary Thomas. Wearing a low cut top, tattered leggings and over caked in make-up, Mary approaches May. She's smoking a long cigarette.
'Are you alright handsome?'
May looks up from staring at the far off sea.
A smiling Mary continues. 'My my, someone's having a bad day. Turn that frown upside down luv. Let Mary give you a good time. I got a room just around the back here.'
May nods and stands up. Mary grabs his hand. 'C'mon lover. I'll give you a night you'll never forget.'

Next morning at Blackpool police Station, twenty four year old, Polish Flight Lieutenant Jan Zumbach. Handsome, dark hair, slim with blue eyes. Zumbach enters into the building and heads to the reception desk.
'I am Flight Lieutenant Jan Zumbach. General Sosabowski has sent me to assist Inspector Appleton in his enquiries.'
Carter notices him and comes across.
He smiles. 'Lieutenant.' The two shake hands.
'I'm Detective Harry Carter. Please come with me.'
Inspector Appleton is sat at the desk in his office when Carter and Zumbach enter. Carter does the introduction.
'Boss, this is Lieutenant Zumbach. The General's liaison.'
Appleton stands and shakes Zumbach's hand.
'We appreciate this Lieutenant.'
Zumbach removes his cap. 'My orders are to help in any manner possible. What exactly do you want from me Inspector?'

'I need to know if any of your men are missing, AWOL since Saturday night?'

Zumbach nods. 'There was one, but he returned this morning. We have him locked up at Squires Gate. But I assure you he is no murderer. This airman is not who you are looking for. '

Appleton stares across at Carter.

'Let us be the judge of that Lieutenant. I'd like Detective Carter to escort you back and interview him. Meanwhile I'll be here speaking to an English soldier who was with the girl shortly before she was killed.'

'He's waiting for you in the interview room,' says Carter. And he's a gibbering wreck.'

Appleton claps his hands together. 'Good. Right then gentlemen, let's get on with it. Off you go.'

Inspector Appleton enters the interview room and sits down facing a nervous looking, uniformed, Eddie Potter. He stares at Potter and lights up a cigarette.

'I'm chief inspector Appleton. You look worried lad. Something you want to tell me?'

Eddie points to the cigarette. 'Can I have one of those?'

Appleton throws him the pack and passes the lighter over the table. Eddie's hands shake badly as he lights up.

'So what happened Eddie?'

'I never did nothing to that girl Mr Appleton. I swear to god, I didn't touch her.'

'You scared of dying Eddie.'

'Why do you ask that?'

'Well chances are you'll be dead in a month or so when Adolf and his boys are goose-stepping up the prom. Did Molly not let you have a piece, so you thought you'd just take it? She struggled; you panicked and killed her, nothing to lose. Am I right?'

Eddie has tears falling down his cheeks.

'No, no way.'

'And to try and get us off your case you thought you'd carve a Swastika onto Molly's forehead?'

An upset Eddie is stunned by this. 'A what? No. Fuckin' ell. No!'

He breaks down in tears.

Appleton appears to takes pity. 'Alright son, calm down. You'll give yourself a heart attack. Now your mate Billy Cardus has an alibi. He got lucky, unlike you. Billy got his end away. He spent the night with Amy Roberts. She confirmed it. Now you need a golden ticket for the Golden fuckin' mile son.

Otherwise, our conversation here goes on and on.'

Eddie takes a huge drag on his cigarette.

'Okay, I picked up a girl.'

Appleton leans across the table. 'What kind of girl. A rubber doll, a hooker, what?'

'She was a prostitute' says Eddie. 'I was drunk. I had a few quid in my pocket. Billy had pissed off with Amy and I didn't want to be on my own. Like you said Inspector. I'll probably be dead soon. A fuckin' German bullet lodged in my head. So I thought, why not?'

'Why didn't you say something before Eddie?'

He looks shamefaced. 'Well I was embarrassed. I thought my Mam and Dad might find out.'

Appleton can't believe what he's hearing. 'Jesus Christ! Right finish your cig, then me and you will go and find this girl and put an end to this.'

'And my Mam and Dad won't have to know?'

Appleton smiles. 'If this girl exists Eddie. No, they will never know. I promise you. Unless you decide to marry her, your secret will be safe with me.'

A relieved Eddie takes a much needed drag on the cigarette. He smiles at his inquisitor. 'Thanks Mr Appleton. I'm really sorry for the trouble.'

'Finish your fag son' sighs Appleton.

'And then we'll go and find your fuckin' Cinderella.'

CALLING CARD

Detective Harry Carter and flight Lieutenant Zumbach enter in a car through the main barrier at Squires Gates. Home to the Polish depot in Blackpool. It is heavily guarded. The guards on duty recognise and salute Zumbach and he returns it.

Sat on a bunk in a holding cell is eighteen year old, Antoni Rosiak. Slim build, blue eyes, blond hair. Carter and Zumbach enter and Rosiak stands to attention. Zumbach smiles towards him. 'At ease Antoni.'

He turns towards Carter. 'Rosiak here speaks perfectly good English, Inspector. So good that he managed to talk a very pretty young girl from Manchester into marrying him on Saturday, after going AWOL on Friday, then reporting back for duty this morning.'

Carter stares at Rosiak.

'Congratulations.'

Rosiak smiles. 'Thank you Sir.'

'I assume you have witnesses?'

'Yes sir. I have my wife. The priest and my new Father and mother-in-law. But they may not be very helpful far as I am concerned.'

'And why's that?' Asks Carter.

'Because they are going to be grandparent's sir. And it was very much a surprise to them.'

Carter tries hard not to laugh. 'I see.'

Zumbach shakes his head. 'Our Romeo here is the only one who did not report back over the weekend. We have made internal enquiries but nothing out of the ordinary has shown itself. We will continue to monitor the men. But regarding that night, everyone else is accounted for.

As for Rosiak? If he is lucky the General will not have him shot because we will need every man when the Germans arrive. He will however be cleaning toilets until they are being used by Nazi arseholes.'

Carter smiles. 'Well thanks for your all your help Lieutenant. I think my time now might be best spent amongst our own rogues and villains in Blackpool's back streets.'

The two men shake hands.

'Then I must accompany you. My General was very specific. Orders are orders.'

I don't think so,' replies Carter.

'You've already done enough. 'Besides,' he starts to laugh. 'I think Blackpool is outside Polish jurisdiction.' Zumbach is not for turning. 'We are on the same side yes? The side of good against evil?'

Carter nods in agreement. He can't help but like the Polish officer.

'I believe we are.'

'Well then Detective' smiles Zumbach. 'Let us go and catch your killer.'

Knowing Zumbach is not going to take no for an answer, Carter gives up.

'You Poles are one hard headed race of bastards, Lieutenant Zumbach. Welcome aboard.'

Zumbach smiles. 'That is why we are still standing Detective.'

At Blackpool police station Detective Harry Carter and Lieutenant Zumbach enter and are immediately greeted by a rushing chief Inspector Appleton on his way out. 'We

have another one Harry. A working girl. Carved up like Molly Gardiner. Come on.'
Appleton stares at Lieutenant Zumbach.
'Nothing to report from Squires Gate boss,' says Carter.
'But the Lieutenant here believes his mandate now extends to helping us find the killer anyway.'
'My orders from General Sosabowski.' Adds Zumbach.
Appleton smiles. 'Well I have no more intentions of upsetting the General again. Welcome to the Blackpool police Lieutenant.'

Appleton, Carter and Zumbach enter into an already packed Mary Thomas's bedroom. Crammed full of uniform and plain clothes policemen.
   Mary lies dead on the bed. Naked, her body bloodied and slashed and cut. On her forehead is carved a Swastika.
'Who found the poor cow?' Asks Appleton.
A constable approaches him. 'One of the other girls boss. Mary hadn't been seen on the street, so they came to look and walked into this mess.'
A commotion is heard outside the bedroom.
 A voice shouting loud. 'Get your bloody hands off me!'
Appleton turns to Carter. 'Go and see what's going on.'
Carter heads into the hallway. There he sees local newspaper reporter Len Hammond. Red-faced, animated and angry.
'Carter what the bloody hell is going on. Have we got another one?'
He nods. 'You can't print this Len. We can't have panic.'
An irate Hammond moves right into Carter's face.
'Now on your say so I kept quiet on the first one. I can't do it again. I have a responsibility to my paper.'
 Carter interrupts. 'First back the fuck off.'

A scared Len moves away.

Carter continues. 'You have a responsibility to the people of Blackpool to keep your mouth firmly shut. You may not have noticed, but we're at war Len. In the middle of a storm that is going to dump on us all.

We can't have people also having to worry about a mass murderer in their midst.

Now the gloves are off. Believe me I've got the authority. You write anything about this and I'll lock you up and find an excuse to throw away the fuckin' key. Okay?'

A grave, ashen face Len nods. 'You win Harry. But I won't forget this.'

He turns and walks away.

Carter enters back into Mary's bedroom. He looks across to Appleton.

'It was Hammond, but I put him straight. He won't be a problem anymore.'

'Good lad. Well Lieutenant You picked a hell of a day to become an honorary Blackpool copper.'

Zumbach smiles. 'Thank you but I have become hardened to death Inspector. When we escaped from Poland, I saw entire villages that had been murdered by the Nazis. Unspeakable things. Whole families hung by wire. Or burned alive in their homes. Machined gunned in ditches. But the Swastika intrigues me. I have seen it before. The Nazi left it at scenes of massacres.

A calling card or in the Jew's case, a Swastika carved on a Rabbi's head.

'So you think the lunatic doing this is German?' Asks Carter.

'Not necessarily. But I think whoever it is wants you to know whose side he's on.'

'No disrespect Lieutenant,' replies Appleton. 'But you don't have to be Sherlock fuckin' Holmes to figure that out. Right now we have to find this mad bastard before he strikes again. Anybody got any ideas?'

Appleton looks around the room at a sea of blank faces. He shakes his head.

'No me neither.'

It is mid-afternoon on Blackpool beach and the sun is shining. Freddie May is walking along the sea edge with trousers rolled up to his ankles. A young boy no more than six approaches. He has a small dog and it is yapping at May's ankles.

The young boy smiles at May. 'It's alright mister he won't bite. All bark and no teeth he is.'

May bends down and goes to stroke it only for the dog to back off and start to growl. The young boy looks surprised.

'Funny, never heard Winston do that before.'

'Noisy little fella ain't he' replies May.

The young boy points at May's face. 'Mister you've got blood on your face.'

May immediately puts a hand on his cheek and washes it in the sea water.

'I cut myself shaving boy. Now be off and take your mutt with you.'

The young boy runs away with the dog chasing after him. May watches as the boy returns to his parents.

He puts a hand back on his face and smiles.

'She felt good.'

SEADOGS

A silver Rolls Royce pulls up outside Seadogs drinking club in the Blackpool backstreets. A ramshackle building with music coming from it.
A half working Neon sign with the A missing, making it *Sedogs.*
 In the Rolls rear is Paddy Owen. Alongside him his bodyguard. Thirty four year old Jimmy 'Scarface' Nolan. A huge man with a former boxer's pug nosed features and a long zig-zag scar that cuts across his cheek.
 Two other large, black suited figures are in the front.
 Nolan looks at the tattered old club and is clearly not impressed.
'Seadogs. What a dump. Who runs this place boss?'
 Owen appears equally unimpressed. 'A weird set up Jimmy.
The manager is a dwarf called Shamus Bigg. He's a former circus act who hates the world and anybody over five feet tall. His sidekick is George Lamb. A nancy boy club singer with a ukulele, who carries a flick knife and prefers to play a tune on that if the chance arises.'
Nolan laughs. 'Only in Blackpool. Sound a right pair of fuckin'charmers.'
Owen smiles. 'You can see for yourself. C'mon time to say hello and do a little charity work for the boys in blue.'
 The four men step out of the car, enter the club and walk down a short corridor into a large dimly lit room. The first sight greeting them at the door is a half-naked, curly haired woman in suspenders, mid-fifties, clearly drunk and sat playing a flute to a nearby vase. Slowly as she plays a

snake starts to rise from it. Owen and his men stare in disbelief.

The woman notices them glaring and hisses in their direction. The snake turns its head also.

'What do you think boss?' Says Nolan. 'Do you want me to shoot that fuckin' thing in case it bites?'

'No shoot the snake instead.'

Nolan takes a revolver from his inside jacket only for Owen to grab it off him.

'Christ you idiot I'm joking!'

They hurry past the woman and her snake. All keeping a safe distance.

The room is half full. Around fifty in all. People's faces lost in the darkness. Some tables are situated in hidden corners, though many are just scattered randomly around. An old black man dressed in a cowboy outfit wearing a white Stetson is sat playing *Summertime* on a piano. On its top is a half drunk bottle of whiskey. He drunkenly hums along to his tune.

They reach the bar. Stood serving is a large bearded man dressed as a woman with a blond wig and a low cut white flowing dress. His face caked in red make-up. He smiles, showing a half mouth of brown stained teeth.

'What can I get you lovely gents?'

'Owen points to the piano player and the swiftly emptying whiskey bottle.

'Just leave one of them on the bar. And when you're done tell Shamus Bigg and George Lamb that Paddy Owen wants a word in their ears. Whilst they still have them.'

Knowing Owen by name only the barman panics. His reputation going well before him. A man to be respected and not messed with.

'Yes sir. I think they are upstairs.'

His hands shaking, he places the bottle and four glasses down.

'Right' says Owen. 'Go and fuckin' fetch him then. And his boyfriend.'

The barman hurries away, lifting up his dress so he doesn't trip.

Owen pours the drinks. 'Help yourself lads.'

He looks around at the clientele. All in various stages of drunkenness and other levels of consciousness. Each desperate not to catch Owen's eye. These are Blackpool's unseen. Allowed through the door at *Seadogs* because nobody else will take their money.

They are renegades, riff-raff, rogues, con men, thieves and every low life known to man. A sea of decadence and debauchery within four walls. This is *Seadogs*. For membership you require only two skills. A licence to do bad and a total disregard for the rules of common decency.

But now as Hitler prepared to unleash hell on earth upon this Sceptre isle even these desperate souls needed companionship. And so they sit and discuss the question on everybody lips in the country. When are the Germans coming? 'Good evening you band of happy few.'

The piano man stops playing and everyone looks towards him.

'You all know me. I'm Patrick Eamonn Owen. Son of Brendan and Shannon Owen. Formerly of the beautiful county off Mayo. Then of Manchester and now of this realm...Blackpool.

Now I'm going to keep this short. Even though the public aren't aware we all know what occurred this last weekend. The young girl found murdered on the beach with the Swastika carved on her forehead.'

A murmur goes around the room.

Owen smiles. 'Ah so you didn't know about that particular fact…

If anyone knows or hears anything, I'm the come to man. No questions asked. I want this fuckin' piece of work dealt with. If not by the boys in blue, then I'll do it. And ladies and gents, here's the big one. I'm offering a ten grand reward to anyone who can deliver this sleezeball to me.' Suddenly another voice cuts across Owen's.

'You've started without me Patrick. How rude.' Appearing from a back room, a most unlikely looking pair. It is forty two year old Shamus Bigg. A dwarf, splendidly and dapper in black suit with a red silk handkerchief in his top pocket. Next to Shamus is his business partner and boyfriend looking equally sartorially elegant. Thirty six year old George Lamb. Slim, skeletal almost, with snake-like eyes and oiled back black hair.

Owen smiles. 'Hello ladies. Long time no see. Care to join us for a drink?' Shamus and George walk over as Owen pours two more whiskeys. He hands them over. 'So you hearing anything?' Shamus shakes his head. 'Nothing. We've not had any strangers in. Just the normal cast of freaks. But there are so many new faces around Blackpool. Who knows what the fuckin' cat has dragged into town.' 'I want this sorted Shamus. Put the word around about the reward. But let it be known I don't want this bastard dead. We need to be sure okay? Ten grand is a lot, I want to make sure I get my money's worth.' 'Since when did you care?' All eyes turn towards the man who has just said this. George Lamb.

'I beg your pardon?' Replies Owen. His bodyguards and Jimmy Nolan stiffening alongside him. Seemingly just waiting for the order to rip Lamb's head from his shoulders.

Lamb stands his ground. 'Just because you want to start acting like a fuckin' priest, why is it our business some little slut has had her throat cut? Are we supposed to care or something?'

Owen motions to Nolan who in turn drops Lamb with a ferocious left hook that sends him reeling to the floor. His nose bursting blood red. A crumpled mess Lamb fumbles in a pocket, but immediately regrets this as Nolan follows with a vicious kick in the ribs. Lamb groans in agony as Harry goes to comfort him.

'I take it you care now George?' Says Owen.

He continues on. 'Now despite appearances around here to the contrary, we are still decent human beings. And before the balloon goes up I won't have Blackpool descend into a pit of filth where anything goes because of what's around the corner.

There are new rules. Number one is we don't hurt our own. Previously I've had no interest into how you lot made a living. If it didn't interfere with mine then so be it, good luck to you. But not anymore. All I can say is this. You dare…You just fuckin' dare and I'll act without mercy.'

Owen motions to his party that it's time to go. He looks across to Shamus who is cradling Lamb in his arms on the floor.

'These are strange times Shamus. The end of days.' Shamus nods as if to agree.

Owen takes out a handkerchief and bends down alongside Lamb. He passes it over. 'Get yourself cleaned up George. You're a lucky boy, if it wasn't for this new era of peace and understanding I would have cut your fuckin' throat myself.'

Owen stands. He straightens his tie and looks around a last time.

'This place needs a makeover Shamus. Be lucky lads and remember what we talked about.'

His piece said Owen turns to leave. On reaching the door he stares at the snake charming lady and winks.

'If you can get mine up like that love you'll have a job for life.'

All smiling they step out of *Seadogs* and back onto the pavement. Owen turns to look at the building. The piano man has started up again.

'Look at the state of this place. It's a health hazard. A rat runs past Owen's feet and back inside the club.

'Remind me Jimmy, if by some miracle the krauts don't arrive we're going to burn this fuckin' hovel to the ground.'

A TERRIBLE, TERRIBLE THING

It is mid-morning and nineteen year old uniformed navy wren, Sally Macdonald, is sat having a cup of tea in a café at the end of Blackpool's north pier. Pretty and petite with blonde hair and blue eyes, this is Sally's last morning before later today being transferred to work in London at the war office. Due to catch the midday train, she has two hours to kill in her home town. The sea is in and Sally can hear the gentle swish of the waves striking below her feet on the pier.

There is only one other person present. A young man sat opposite. His table ten yards from Sally's. He looks across and catches her eye.

She smiles but the young man puts his head down.

Deciding to leave Sally goes to pay, only to suffer a feeling of panic when realising she can't find her purse. Behind the counter an old lady with stern features and cold eyes is not impressed.

'I'm not stood waiting for the good of my health young girl. What seems to be the problem?'

Sally looks up from her handbag. 'I'm so sorry I can't find my purse?'

'Quite' smiles the old lady. 'A likely story.'

A voice speaks up behind them.

'I'll pay for it.' Sally turns around. It is Freddie May.

'Thank you' smiles a startled Sally.

May hands the old woman the money.

She continues. 'I'll pay you back, but my train ticket was also in the purse.

I'm due to report for duty in London this evening. If I don't turn up I'll be in terrible trouble.'

May smiles. 'What time does your train leave?'

Sally is close to tears. 'In two hours.'

'I'll tell you what we'll do' replies May.

'We'll retrace your steps and if it doesn't turn up, I'll lend you the money for another ticket, and you can mail it me back when you have it.

I only live a short distance away, so we can just nip back there for the money. Okay?'

Sally smiles and nods. 'You are so kind.' She takes outs a tissue and blows her nose.

'Now dry your eyes and don't worry,' says May. 'Everything will be alright.'

Inspector Sydney Appleton is sat in office when the door suddenly swings open and there stands Detective Harry Carter.

'No one ever teach you to knock Carter?' Appleton notices that he looks ashen faced.

'What's up, you look like you've seen a ghost?'

'We've got another one boss.'

Appleton leans back in his chair. 'Where?'

'A nineteen year old navy wren. Sally Macdonald. Two schoolboys found her body in a back alley. Just off the north pier.'

'What no witnesses? There's thousands of people milling around there at any one time?'

'He'd cut the body up and put it in binbags. The bastard had beheaded her. Some schoolboys noticed dogs sniffing around it.'

Appleton is aghast. 'And the Swastika? Was it?'

Carter nods. 'It's him.'

Appleton stands and grabs his coat and trilby. 'C'mon let's get down there.'

As the Policemen leave the station Flight Lieutenant Zumbach is arriving.

Harry puts three fingers up at him and Zumbach shakes his head.

'Another?'

'Would you care to join us Lieutenant. l hate to say but this is becoming a daily occurrence.'

Hundreds of people are milling around the crime scene as the car carrying Appleton, Carter and Zumbach arrives. Word has spread swift around the town. Already rumours have been rife about a mass murderer on the loose. This just seems to confirm it.

Police constables stand in a line attempting to hold back the ever increasing crowds. The alley way swarms with investigating officers. Both uniformed and plain. An angry Appleton is almost apoplectic with rage at these scenes.

'This is not a fuckin' house of horrors at the funfair. No one is selling tickets. Get these people away.'

The constables start to push the hordes of onlookers back.

'Appleton turns to Carter. 'Take our Polish friend here and go and check on the pier. Ask around.'

'Yes boss' replies Carter.

Appleton heads towards the scene of the body. A constable approaches him.

'Sir we found the girl's handbag. She had no family. Raised in an orphanage. There's a priest.'

The constable points across to a figure kneeling over the body parts. He is making the sign of the cross.

'Who's that'? Asks Appleton.

'That's Father Mallon. He knew Sally. She was in his church chorus. Did the readings every Sunday.'

Appleton goes across. The priest stands and places rosary beads back in his pocket.

'Father I'm Chief Inspector Appleton.'

The two men shake hands.

'I need to ask. When did you last see Sally alive?'

'Sunday morning at mass. She was going away yesterday to London. Sally was so excited. She had been chosen to work as a telephonist at the war office. I knew she was due to get the twelve o'clock train yesterday afternoon. For I was going to surprise and see her off. She had nobody you see. A beautiful simple girl who just wanted to help her country in its time of need. A terrible, terrible thing this Inspector. You must catch this man. You must.'

'We will Father. I promise.'

A scuffle in the crowd is heard behind them and the old lady who works at the pier café appears at the front of the scrum.

She is shouting and trying to manhandle her way through the police line.

'Let me through. Let me through now!'

Appleton goes to walks towards her, only for Father Mallon to tap him on his shoulder.

He is holding a photograph of Sally.

'Take this. Hopefully it may help.'

'Thank you.'

Appleton faces the old lady. He motions to the constable holding her back to let go. She pushes through.

'Now what can we do for you?' Asks Appleton.

'I heard the girl murdered was a Navy wren. Yesterday morning a young lass like that was in my café. She'd lost her purse and couldn't pay. There was a man there. He volunteered to pay for her.'

Appleton shows the old lady the photograph.

'Oh my good that's her.' She breaks down in tears.

'You say a man was with her?' Appleton's heart jumps a beat.

'I need you to come to the station straight away with me love. Okay. Now what's your name?'

Sobbing the old lady accepts a tissue off Appleton to dry her eyes.

'Margaret Watkins.'

Well Margaret Watkins, you've just become the most important person in Blackpool.'

Appleton places an arm around Margaret and they walk over to the car.

'C'mon love.'

The car drives off.

SIEG HEIL

A constable races up the pier to pass word to Carter and Zumbach of Margaret Watkins.

'We best get back' says Carter. 'See how the boss wants to play this.'

Zumbach doesn't reply. His eyes are focused on a man watching them across the pier. It is a smiling Freddie May. Zumbach point across 'Harry look over there?'

May is stood staring. He waves across and starts to laugh loud.

Carter is getting angry. 'What's his problem?'

They walk across to confront May. He stops laughing.

'What's so funny?' Asks Carter.

'Everything' replies May.

'What do you mean everything?' Says Zumbach.

'What is your problem?' Snaps Carter.

'It's just too easy.' May puts out both his arms. 'Take me in, I'm bored.'

Carter looks at Zumbach in astonishment

'Take you in. What for?'

'Are you stupid? What do you think?'

A stunned Carter is momentarily at a loss for words.

'Are you saying you killed the girls.'

May smiles wide. 'Congratulation Detective. The suns shines through the fuckin' trees at last. Now are you going to arrest me or do I have to kill another?'

'Tell me something about the girls?' Asks Carter.

You mean the Swastika? The blonde girl under here? Oh she screamed until I had finished my work. Then the old slag. That was messy. And last but not least our young and beautiful wren. That was the hardest of the three. She cried a lot till I shut her mouth by cutting off her fuckin' head.'

Zumbach immediately lunges at May, whilst Carter handcuffs him.

May starts to laugh again. 'Oh you have no idea what is going to happen next. No idea. Sieg Heil, Sieg Heil.'

Carter and Zumbach drag him off the pier with May laughing all the way.

Blackpool police station is in lockdown. A ring of constables surround the building to keep out prying journalist and photographers. Chief Inspector Appleton is with Margaret Watkins as she confirms through a peephole in a holding cell door that the man she saw with Sally was Freddie May.

'That's him' she says. ' That's the bastard.'

'Appleton smiles. 'Thank you for everything. I'll arrange for one of my officers to drive you home.'

A constable takes her away, leaving Appleton stood with Carter and Zumbach. 'Right' exclaims Appleton! He claps his hands together and gazes through the peephole at May.

'Time to go to work.'

Inspector Appleton' says Zumbach. 'I think my time amongst you is done. I will return to General Sosabowski and inform him that we are fighting alongside good and honest men.'

Zumbach hold out his hand and Appleton accepts.

'Thanks for everything' says Appleton. 'Give my regards to the General.' Lieutenant Zumbach shakes hands also with Detective Carter.

'Good luck Lieutenant' says Carter.

'Thank you. Hopefully there will be happier times when we can all sit down and drink a toast to the friendship between our two great nations.'

Appleton smiles. 'I'll look forward to that day and hold you to it Flight Lieutenant.'

Zumbach salutes the two policemen and walks off down the corridor.

They watch him go. 'A good lad' says Appleton.

'But if he thinks there will be happier times then whatever they put in the Polish vodka is far stronger than the stuff in mine.'

He puts an arm around Carter's shoulders.

'C'mon Harry, let's go and nail this bastard.'

ABSOLUTION OF SIN

Appleton and Carter are sat facing Freddie May. His is a thousand mile stare.

'Well May' smiles Appleton. 'I'm already looking forward to the day you swing.'

'I'm not going to hang Mr Appleton.' Replies a smiling May.

'Oh yes you are lad. They are going to put a sack over your head and as I watch you fall through that fuckin' trap door, I'll raise a glass and smile when your neck snaps. '

May shakes his head. 'Does either of you gentlemen play cards?'

'I enjoy a game of poker' replies Carter. 'But what has that got to do with anything?'

'Well then you'll know that all life is a game of chance. You play it with a straight face and a poker smile. No matter how strong or powerful, rich or poor, everyone, sometimes, needs a get out of jail card.

Isn't that right Mr Carter?'

'Go on.'

A smiling May leans over the table towards the two policemen.

'Well me. I've been born, no blessed. Though some from these parts may claim cursed with the wings of an avenging angel. One you know well. I'm such a fuckin' lucky man. Look at me. I can smile like the man who broke the bank at Monte Carlo.

Or who ended up with the best looking girl at the wedding.

I ride an invisible cloud. I dance with fallen angels. I am untouchable. The son of a living God who hates your fuckin' guts.'

'What are you talking about May?' Replies Appleton. Swiftly losing patience.

'You've admitted the crimes. We have a witness. We have the girl's blood found in your room. You're already on the gallows. You're deluded son and are going to pay for your crimes.'

Again May smiles. 'The trials and tribulations of our childhood Mr Appleton. None of us can help who our parents are. We're born into this cruel world without knowledge or the power to change our fate. A boy growing up without a father in Liverpool. A mother who always blamed me for him leaving without a simple goodbye. Not a word or a letter. Christ it's not as if he can't talk or pen a fuckin' line?'

Appleton stands. He turns his back on May for a second, and then faces him again. 'Just where are we going with this Freddie? Do you want sympathy, is that it? Poor little scouse boy driven to acts of murder because his mum didn't like him and his dad did a runner. It isn't going to wash with me or the judge. There can be no salvation.

You're pure evil. A fuckin' pestilence in all our lives when we need it least with all that's brewing.'

'Do you know anything of the absolution of sin Mr Appleton?'

Appleton nods. 'I was raised a Catholic, what of it?'

May nods. 'I thought so. An altar boy? Did you get to serve the priest in all of God's need Inspector? Did you get down on your knees for him?'

Appleton is fighting hard to stay calm. 'You're not getting inside my head May. But just so you know, you're one more measly comment from receiving the beating of your miserable, pitiable life.'

May smiles. 'Well then you'll know no matter how horrendous the sin, if you beg the almighty for forgiveness hard enough, you'll be granted entrance to the kingdom of heaven.

Maybe not through the front door and you may have to spend your life saying a million fuckin' Hail Mary's, but in the end, if you repent hard enough they'll fall for it, and hey!
You're family again.'

'Get it off your chest Freddie,' says Carter. 'Whatever it is you're desperate to tell us. Speak up, let's hear it?'
May shakes his head. 'You think I've come this far to make it that easy for you Mr Carter?'
 Suddenly an outraged Appleton grabs May by the throat and has him against the cell wall.

'You would do well to remember I've seen you handiwork May. Now there's a war on and if you wish to spend just a little more time on this earth before we end you, then cut out this bull. Do I make myself clear?'
 Inches from Appleton's face, May smiles. 'You still don't get it do you. I'm like the waves that crash forever onto Blackpool's beach. No matter how hard you try, you'll never be able to stop me. My power is beyond your comprehension.

Now the game truly begins with me giving you a clue as to what you're up against. Send your man here to Liverpool.'
May points to Carter.
'Have him find my, want for of a better word, mother. Let her tell the world just what she let inside her twenty seven years ago.'

'Okay then Freddie' smiles Appleton. 'We'll play along with this charade of yours for a day or two. God knows every dead man walking deserves a last day in the Blackpool sun. I'll buy you a stick of rock and you can suck on it whilst contemplating your last goodbye.'

May drinks a glass of water then places it back on the table. He stares at Carter, who secretly believes he's seen his face somewhere before. But just can't trace it.

'Well let the game begin' says May.

His eyes like daggers at the two policemen.

'Let the game begin.'

It is early evening and dark clouds are hovering over Blackpool. The days of summer appear over. Appleton and Carter are walking along the prom eating fish and chips out of newspaper.

'I want you to go to Liverpool Harry. Talk to May's Mother. Find out just what the hell he's hinting at.'

'He's just playing for time if you ask me boss. May knows the court won't mess around to see him off. The sooner the better for all concerned.'

'But why give himself up?' Exclaims an exasperated Appleton.

'It doesn't make sense. He obviously doesn't have a death wish.

No there's something not quite right.'

'Do you want me to bring her back?' Asks Carter.

'Her choice' replies Appleton. 'But listen Harry, Liverpool is getting bombed off the face of the earth. The Germans are hitting the ports with everything they've got. It's been going on for two weeks. You won't be reading about it in the papers because of a news blackout, but the city is being razed to the ground. There's God knows how many dead. So just be prepared for what you are walking into.'

IT'S NOT THE LEAVING OF LIVERPOOL

A city on fire: Liverpool, along with Birkenhead is the largest seaport on the English west coast and Herman Goering's Luftwaffe is pulverising it night after night. The bombings are heavy and sustained and the casualties are horrendous. Being of incalculable importance to the British war effort, the government is concealing both from its own people and the Germans just how much damage is being inflicted on the docks and surrounding areas. It is rumoured the death toll is already in the thousands.

The sirens first resonated out across Liverpool on the night of 28th August 1940, when 160 bombers came in over the Atlantic. This assault continued over the next three nights as a red haze settled over the ravaged city. Air wardens fighting desperately to stem the fires that raged wildly out of control. The waters of the Mersey proving a lifeline as the bombs fell many times off target and flattening amongst other things. Air raid shelters, churches. And on one heart-breaking occasion, hitting a maternity ward in a hospital, killing all the mothers and babies. This was the blitz.

The Liverpool blitz of 1940.

And this was the city Detective Harry Carter arrived in during these early September days.

Making his way down a bomb devastated, rubble-strewn, terraced, backstreet, Carter looks at a piece of paper in his hand.

On it reads *21 Stanhope Street. Toxteth.*

A little girl no more than five, clutching a rag doll, her face etched in dirt stares at Carter with eyes that have seen far too much, for one so young.

He smiles but she doesn't return it. A woman appears from a doorway and grabs her hand.

She too glares at Carter before disappearing back inside with the girl.

A full quarter of the street has been destroyed in the bombing, but Carter notices number 21 is still standing. He makes his way towards the door and knocks on.

The sound of a latch being released on the door and Katherine May appears.

Forty eight years old, clearly once beautiful, now her face creased with worry lines. Her hair once black now more grey, with eyes sat on sagging skin that in itself spoke volumes to say this woman has suffered a life few could imagine.

Katherine almost spits out the words. 'What do you want?'

'Miss Katherine May? 'Asks Carter.

'She nods. 'What is it to you?'

'I have news regarding your son.'

Suddenly Katherine's entire demeanour changes.

'Where is he? Is he okay?' Immediately tears form in Katherine's eyes.

'May I come in please?'

She opens the door.

Katherine leads Carter into a small living room. He notices the many photographs of Freddie May as a child on her walls. It is a tidy room. A bookshelf with titles such as Charles Dickens and the works of William Shakespeare amongst other classics adorn it.

'Tell me about my son?'

'You may want to sit down.'

She does so. 'Now go on' replies Katherine. Clearly bracing herself for the worse.

'I'm afraid to tell you Freddie has been arrested for the murder of three women. He is currently being held at Blackpool police station awaiting trial.'

Katherine puts her hand over her mouth to prevent screaming out loud.

'He's already admitted his guilt Miss May. It's now just a question of justice taking its course.'

A distraught Katherine looks pleadingly at Carter. 'My son is not a monster detective. He isn't capable of such evil.'

Carter shakes his head. There's no mistake and no doubt. He's committed these grave acts and we have irrefutable evidence.

Freddie himself is not disputing the fact. He's even boasting about what he's done.'

Katherine appears in shock.

'But there's something else.'

She looks up.

'Freddie spoke about his father?'

'Forget his father' snaps Katherine. 'He never had one. He left this city many years ago and doesn't even know Freddie exists. The leaving of Liverpool it turned out was the making of him. He's become many things but never a father.'

'We all had one Miss May. It's simply some were better than others. Freddie seems to believe the reasons for his actions is down to him. And is under the crazy notion that even now his father will save him from the noose.

'Who was he? It's important in our enquiries that we establish this fact.'

Katherine has stopped crying. She blows her nose and attempts to steady herself.

Katherine looks Carter direct in the eyes.

You must understand that what I'm about to tell you. I've never spoken about to anyone. Apart from Freddie.'

'Who is he Miss May?'

'Freddie's father is Adolf Hitler.'

PATIENCE OF ANGELS

Inspector Appleton is sat at his desk trying to take in what Harry Carter has just informed him.

'Harry this is fuckin' crazy. Freddie May's father is Adolf Hitler? The woman was obviously drunk. Or at best deluded.'

'I don't think so boss' replies Harry. He takes a small photograph out of his pocket and hands it to Appleton. It shows a young Katherine May with a twenty three year old Adolf Hitler. On the back is written *Liverpool November 1912.* Hitler could well be Freddie's twin.

Harry continues. 'At that time Hitler was a struggling painter. He came to Liverpool from Vienna to try and avoid military conscription. The war was brewing and the authorities had him earmarked for the military. So our Adolf jumped on a boat to England. Quite ironic don't you think. He was over here living in Toxteth for six months when Katherine May enters the story.

A brief fling took place and hence the result twenty yards down the corridor. Freddie May. A love child. The title doesn't really do him justice does it? Anyway due to money problems and him not having any,

Hitler returned to Vienna in April of the following year. Katherine swears blind he knew nothing of the baby.

Freddie himself only found out a few months ago. She'd always told him his old man was a Russian sailor. Rather than the mad Nazi Fuhrer now seemingly intent on taking over the world'

'I think I need a drink. So what happened?' Asks a stunned Appleton

Carter points to the picture in Appleton's hand.
'He found that. Look at him boss. They could be twins. So Freddie put two and two together, confronted Katherine and she confirmed it. He disappeared that very day and she'd not heard of him since. Until yesterday when I turned up with the grim tidings.'
Appleton looks at the picture once more. In the background are Liverpool docks with huge cargo ships being unloaded. Both Katherine and Hitler are smiling and appearing like any other courting young couple.
'Well Freddie's definitely picked up Dad's penchant for mass murder.'
Appleton is clearly reeling at what he's just been told.
'Where do we go with this? Hitler's son? It's definitely out of our league Harry. I'm going to contact the war office. Get their people here.
In the meantime, if by some fluke this gets out we're going to have a riot on our hands. A pathological killer who has murdered three innocent local women is bad enough. But this?
Jesus Christ, they'll hang him high from the top of the fuckin' tower.
Harry, I want you to place a twenty four watch on May. Two men at all times. Nobody speaks to him without my say so.'
Carter nods. 'Will do.'
'Nobody else can know about this. The less the better. And sorry to curtail your social life, but me and you are sleeping here until May is safely ensconced in military hands.'
Appleton opens his draw and takes out a revolver. He hands it to Carter.

'Now keep this on you at all times. I don't want you playing Roy Rodgers with it, but if the need arises and you feel obliged to then go ahead.

There's a war on after all. Do you understand me?'

Carter smiles. Don't worry. I've got this.'

'Good man' replies Appleton.

Ten Downing Street: London: The Prime Minister Winston Churchill is sat in his office when a knock on the door and one of his inner circle, thirty eight year old Major James Willard appears. Cambridge born and educated. Tall with receding hair and slim moustache. A man with a warm but commanding presence.

'Prime Minister we have a situation in Blackpool.'

Churchill lights up a cigar and pours himself a whiskey from a bottle on his desk. 'What kind of situation Major?'

'I fear you best have your drink first sir.'

The Prime Minister takes a large sip of his whiskey.

'Now I've done as you asked Willard. Get on with it man.'

The war office received a call around twenty minutes ago from a Chief Inspector Appleton of the Blackpool police.'

Willard appears hesitant.

An impatient Churchill rolls his eyes. 'Spit it out man.'

'Well sir, two days ago they arrested a young man from Liverpool by the name of Freddie May, for the murder of three young women.

In the cause of their investigations it led them back to Liverpool and May's mother. It turns out that this man is the son of one Adolf Hitler.'

A shocked Churchill finishes his whiskey glass. 'Are we absolutely one hundred per cent on this Major?'

'It appears so. What would you have me do?'

'I wish to speak to this Inspector Appleton. Arrange a call for me now.'

'Yes Prime Minister.'

'Also have MI6 fly two of their best men north to bring this fellow May to London.'

'Do you have something in mind sir?'

Churchill stands and looks out his window. Appearing deep in thought, he gazes up at the barrage balloons that covet the London sky.

'We have all but nothing to bargain with against Herr Hitler at the moment Major. Sometimes fate throws you a bone or a scrap that just might prove invaluable. Who knows?'

He turns to face Major Willard and smiles. 'Now get me that Blackpool policeman on the line.'

'Yes sir' replies Willard.

Inspector Appleton is on the verge of leaving his office when the phone rings. He picks it up. 'Hello'

A woman's voice answers. 'Is that Chief Inspector Sydney Appleton of Blackpool Police?'

'It is, who's this?'

'Please hold for the Prime Minister, Inspector.'

Appleton takes a deep breath and sits down at his desk. Churchill comes on the line. 'Good day to you Inspector Appleton.'

'Good day sir.'

First I would like to commend you on your excellent work in apprehending this vile criminal Freddie May.'

'Thank you.'

And secondly you must ensure no harm comes to him before my people arrive in the next couple of hours. This is a matter of grave national security Inspector Appleton. I cannot stress enough, even though this man's actions are truly monstrous, we need him alive and well here in London.'

'I have two constables and my best detective watching him at all times sir. He's safe enough until we hang him.'

Churchill's line goes momentarily quiet, making Appleton think he's been cut off. Only for the Prime Minister to then continue.

'You must do your duty Inspector. Do we understand each other?'

'Absolutely sir' replies Appleton.

The line goes dead and he puts down the phone.

Carter enters and notices the utter bemusement on his Inspector's face.

'Who was that?'

'The big man himself. Winston Churchill. Our friend is to be transferred to London. Until then he's our responsibility. But something is troubling me Harry.'

'What is it?'

'It doesn't feel right. Justice has to be served. Not even the patience of angels would be enough to grant this monster any kind of redemption. Surely?'

Carter appears confused. 'You've lost me now boss.'

'Well I believe London has something else in mind for Freddie May.'

'Such as?' Replies Carter.

Appleton ignores Carter's question.

He smiles. 'C'mon, let's go and check on the prisoner. Mr Frederick Hitler.'

THE PROMISE

Appleton and Carter stand facing Freddie May in his holding cell. May is sat down and smoking. He smiles on seeing them enter. Appleton nods to the constable with him to leave the room.

He does so as both detectives pull up chairs.

'So' begins May. 'My big secret is out I take it?'

You'll be on a plane to London within a couple of hours' replies Appleton.

'Hopefully then the next time we meet I'll be watching you swing.'

'Your mother doesn't want to see you May' adds Carter. 'You've broke her heart?'

'And that is supposed to upset me Mr Carter? That woman lied to me for years about who my father was. It's down to her why I killed. She denied me the chance of being by his side.'

You're blaming your mother for what you did to those poor women?

Carter shakes his head. 'I can't listen to any more of this.' He looks across to Appleton who nods and Carter leaves the room.

May watches him go. 'He's weak Mr Appleton. When my father's army arrives on these shores people like him will be disposed of.'

Oh is this the Nazi master race we keep hearing about. Well one look at you and your old man and you're not exactly Flash fuckin' Gordon are you?'

May smiles. 'You best be nice to me Chief Inspector. There may well come a day when I'm stood where you are deciding whether you live or die.'

Appleton shakes his head. 'Let's get one thing straight May. Even if the Germans do invade and your old man is giving it the big one from the Buckingham Palace balcony, it'll make no difference to you. Because I swear to God if the authorities somehow make a decision to keep you alive, then I'll kill you myself.'

Such is the Chief Inspector's mad look in his eyes, May says nothing. He simply stares. Appleton goes to leave, only to turn around a last time.

'The three reasons I intend to keep this promise are simple.

They are Molly Gardiner, Mary Thomas and Sally Macdonald.'

Later that evening at Squires gate a lone RAF transport plane comes into land on the runway. On board are M16 agents, thirty three year old Robert Morley. Balding, small, but well built. And thirty five year old Matthew Stephens. Black sleeked, well-groomed hair, handsome and slim.

Both men are met on the tarmac by Flight Lieutenant Jan Zumbach who has orders to drive them to the police station.

He offers his hand and both men shake it.

'Welcome to Blackpool gentlemen.'

Zumbach smiles. 'I am Flight Lieutenant Zumbach. Please follow me.'

He leads Morley and Stephens over to an army jeep where they climb into the rear, whilst Zumbach jumps in the driving seat.

'The policemen Appleton and Carter are good men' he says.
 Morley stares across Stephens.
 'Do you know them both well then Lieutenant?' Asks Morley.
'I worked as a liaison officer during the investigation to capture Freddie May.' Suddenly both M16 men appear wary. Stephens eyes Zumbach like a leopard preparing to rip the throat of a cornered deer.
'How much are you aware of what is occurring?'
'I don't understand?' Replies a quizzical Zumbach.
'Best you just take us to the police station,' snaps Morley.
'And say nothing more about it, Lieutenant. Just forget anything that you have seen or heard over the last few days.
That's a fucking order. Do you understand?'
Zumbach glances back at him through a rear mirror but says nothing. Instead he just starts the jeep and they drive off.

After a short journey through town they pull up outside the station.
Morley and Stephens step out of the jeep.
'You wait here Lieutenant,' says Morley. Zumbach again remains silent. Intrigued as to what is occurring.
 On entering they are met by Detective Carter. 'Gentlemen please follow me.'
Carter takes them to Appleton's office, who stands from his desk.
'Welcome to Blackpool' smiles Appleton. Shaking both their hands.
 'Thank you Inspector. I am agent Morley, this here is Stephens.

We are from M16 and have orders to take the prisoner Freddie May back to London, soon as possible.'

Appleton smiles. 'MI6. There's me thinking it only went up to five?'

'It does' replies a grim faced Stephens.

'Now we have been assured of your full co-operation on this matter.'

'Of course' says Appleton. 'I'll arrange for May's transfer straight away.'

'One small thing' adds Morley.

'The Polish officer in the jeep outside. Is he aware of May's true identity?'

'No' replies Carter. 'The Lieutenant helped out on the enquiry, but returned back to normal duties before the link with Hitler was established.'

Morley addresses the two policemen.

'I must warn you Inspector Appleton, and you too Detective Carter. That from this moment on you are both subject to the *Official Secrets Act*. Any mention of this matter to others and you can be arrested for high treason and executed. Do I make myself clear?'

'I know my duty Agent Morley' replies a stern faced Appleton.

'As does Detective Carter here. There's no need for threats. Your secret is safe.

LONDON'S BURNING

In the beginning, the Luftwaffe target RAF airfields and radar stations for destruction, in preparation for the forthcoming German invasion of the island. Operation *Sea lion*. Their armies lie in wait across the English Channel. Once the RAF has been dealt a critical blow and the skies belonged to Germany it can begin. The Luftwaffe bombers first appear in the skies over the capital on the afternoon of September 7, 1940. This heralds a tactical shift in Adolf Hitler's attempt to subdue Great Britain. His patience with Winston Churchill is exhausted. The RAF's revenge attacks on Berlin and the fact Churchill has poured scorn on every olive branch offered by Hitler has seen him change tact. And so the Fuhrer now resorts to type and unleashes hell from the skies on Britain's major industrial cities.

None more than London is now feeling his wrath.

At around 4:00 PM on this bright September day, 348 German bombers, escorted by 617 fighters come to raze London to the ground. The city is swiftly ringed in flames and stabbed constantly with fire. The planes are heard grinding overhead and the boom of the ack ack guns start up in retaliation.

An orange red haze is soon lighting up the entire horizon.

The ferocity of the explosions are savage beyond words.

The crackling flames, the smell of charred, lit wood. The countless corpses lying black and unrecognisable. Body parts reduced to cinders.

The screams of the injured and the yelling of firemen and air wardens. An incessant battle with their hoses. Like firing water pistols to douse an angry volcano.

Small fires turning into infernos. London is burning. Above the bombs still fall. Every two minutes a new wave of planes are arriving. Their engines a constant moan. Like a million bees buzzing in furious irritation. Whole batches of incendiary bombs on parachutes that flash simmer and turn white, then setting alight another building.
It never ends.

Smoke billowing across the capital. And through it all untouched, as if by magic or sheer luck it matters little. The great dome of St. Paul's Cathedral. Surrounded by fire and yet? It just stands there.
Defiant. As if urging the Luftwaffe to do your best.

Finally their blood lust satisfied the German turn and go home. But they will be back. Again and again. The Battle of Britain is raging and the British are losing…

East End London: Prime Minister Winston Churchill is walking amongst the rubble of a London street that has been devastated by German bombs. Alongside him his aide Major James Willard and a huddle of local politicians. Around them hundreds of locals have gathered. They appear in utter shock at what has befallen them. Churchill's armed bodyguards stiffen, but there appears no animosity towards the Prime Minister. A young girl no more than six, wearing a pretty flowered dress, breaks rank and races towards Churchill with a small bunch of half dead daffodils in hand.

He motions for her to be allowed through his security. Churchill bends down so he is eye level with the girl. She smiles and hands him the flowers.

'Thank you young lady' he says. 'What's your name?'
'Caroline. My daddy was killed in a place called Dunkirk.
But my mummy says you will make everything all right
again.'

Churchill gives the girl a small hug, and then stands as
the entire crowd cheer and applaud him. He gives them a
victory salute. Inside though he fears greatly for Churchill
knows the horrors that still awaits these people. His
people.
Bombed to oblivion and then almost certainly being forced
to live under the Nazi jackboot when the invasion arrives.
He has made up his mind.
Churchill turns to Major Willard. 'You my young man are
going on a small journey for me.'
 'Where to sir?' He asks.
'Berlin' replies Churchill.
Willard doesn't reply for he is simply too shocked to open
his mouth.

BERLIN

Berlin: 76/78 Tirpitzufer: Abwehr Intelligence Headquarters: Fifty three year old, silver haired, Head of *Abwehr*, Admiral Wilhelm Canaris, is in his office when there is a frantic knock at his door. It is twenty four year old, blond haired Oberleutnant Franz Muller. He gives a Nazi salute.
Canaris who is no fan of the Fuhrer looks up in disdain at Muller.
He smiles. 'Come now Franz, enough of that. What do you have for me?'
Muller hands Canaris a telex which he reads out loud:
…'It is in Herr Hitler's interest not to bomb the Tower of London until further notice...Katherine May says hello'...
  Canaris appears perplexed. 'What is this gibberish?'
'We received it off MI6 ten minutes ago sir. It is a direct contact.'
Get me a meeting with Hitler right away.'
Muller goes to give another Nazi salute then stops halfway when noticing he is being glared at by Canaris. Muller resorts to a normal salute which is returned by the Admiral. He leaves the room. Canaris stares once more at the telex. 'What is this all about?'

Reich Chancellery: It is early evening and The Fuhrer, fifty one year old Adolf Hitler is sat in an armchair by an open fire in his luxurious private quarters. He is reading a host of documents piled high before him. All is not going to plan in the skies over England. The unexpected resistance of the RAF and the bravery, skill and sheer audacity of their spitfire and Hurricane pilots are causing heavy losses amongst Hermann Goring's Luftwaffe bombers.

What appeared a simple matter of when is swiftly becoming a big if? If air superiority cannot be achieved Operation *Sea lion* is in serious trouble of being postponed. Hitler flicks through the latest reports. All bad. His mood darkening. To this brooding atmosphere, Admiral Canaris knocks and enters. He gives the Nazi salute. Hating himself whilst doing so.
Hitler smiles on seeing the Admiral. 'Wilhelm come, come. It is good to see you.'

Hitler rises. 'Come and sit beside me.' He points to a facing armchair.
Canaris heads over and hands Hitler the telex.

'My Fuhrer, we received this message from British M16. It is marked for your attention.' Hitler reads it then creases up the piece of paper in his fist.

He turns to Canaris. His eyes disbelieving and clearly reeling. 'How many people have seen this?'
'Only two others my Fuhrer. An officer on my staff and a telex operator.'
'Tell them from me. If a word of this is mentioned to anyone they will be executed.'

'Of course but it is not necessary' replies Canaris. 'I trust all who work under me with my life. I would never doubt their loyalty to me and more importantly to you.'

Hitler stares at Canaris. He nods, and then sits back down. His mind racing with thoughts of Katherine May and once upon a time in Liverpool.
Canaris sits. 'What is happening my Fuhrer? How can I help?'

Hitler suddenly switches back to the present. 'Tell Goering to issue orders that The Tower of London must not be bombed. It is out of bounds. Stress this to him and God help any pilot or their families who disobeys me. Go now there is no time to waste.'

Canaris stands and starts to make his way to the door. Hitler shouts out. 'Wilhelm.'

He turns around. 'Yes my fuhrer.'

'Get back in touch with the English. Tell them they have my undivided attention.' Canaris nods in recognition of this and leaves. Whatever just occurred he knows has rocked Hitler to the core. The Admiral is intrigued as to the name of the woman, Katherine May.

Just who is she?

Tower of London: Flanked by MI6 agents Morley and Stephens, and two armed soldier both rear and front, a handcuffed Freddie May is led into the tower of London. He is quiet and has not spoken a word since landing from Blackpool.

Once inside May's handcuffs are taken off and he is taken to a cell. A red cap military policeman already stands on guard. He's holding across his chest a sub machine gun. The door is unlocked and Morley and Stephens take May inside. He looks around at its grim interior.

'He'll come for me' says a smiling May. 'Sooner or later he'll knock these fuckin' walls down and he'll come for me.'

Both the agents simply stare and say nothing. Suddenly the air raid sirens resonate loud outside.

Morley laughs. 'This could be him now.'

On hearing this Stephens is also grinning wide.

'We'll leave you alone now May' says Stephens. 'Off to the shelter you see. Where it's safe.'

May starts to panic. 'You can't just leave me here?'

The agents leave, the cell door being slammed behind them. They can hear May still shouting. Screaming abuse.

'We received word from Berlin an hour ago' says Morley.

'The Germans confirmed they received the telex and have agreed not to bomb the tower. But no need to let this murdering bastard know.'

They walk away smiling.

Ten Downing Street: In Winston Churchill's office Major James Willard is sat facing his Prime Minister. He has just been informed the reason for his trip to Berlin. Churchill is giving him time for it to sink in. He gets up and goes to pour two whiskeys for himself and the Major.

'So let me get this straight sir' says Willard.

'You want me to go to Berlin, have a meeting with Adolf Hitler and inform him in exchange for not invading, we are willing to hand over the son he never knew existed?'

A smiling Churchill hands him his whiskey. 'That's about it Major. Yes.

And be clear to tell Herr Hitler that if he does not agree, then I shall hang him from the highest petard for all see. We will film it and I shall tell the world of his heinous crimes and whose this bastard's father really is.'

'With great respect Sir. This is absolutely mad.'

'I totally agree' says the Prime Minister.

'Absolutely outrageous if you ask me. But we are going to lose this war James. I can make all the speeches in the world about drowning in our own blood and fighting them on the beaches, but the truth is our army lost all its equipment on the beaches of Dunkirk. We are hopelessly outgunned.

Never in courage and heart, but where it matters most. In armaments.

Now we are never going to surrender. We shall throw everything we have at the bastards when they come. From poison gas to clubs and knives. From the highlands of Scotland to the rolling green fields of Surrey, our blood will flow in a last stand.

But this? Mad as it may sound, is a gift from a guilty feeling God.

This monster Freddie May has given me an option I never thought would arise. A chance, slight maybe, that Herr Hitler has beneath that evil demeanour, a beating fucking heart of a father.

So we are going to try Major Willard. I need you to believe in this plan. I need you to make Hitler believe. Because if this fails then England, Great Britain, as we have known her will cease to exist and became a Nazi state. A gigantic graveyard for I will not allow us to go gently into the German night. So believe what you are telling him Major Willard.

Believe.'

Churchill smiles. 'And now drink your whiskey.'

Willard does so, quite convinced the Prime Minister has lost his mind. But he will do as ordered and try with all his might to ensure the old man's words about this country becoming a gigantic graveyard do not come to fruition.

GYPSY LADY

Katherine May walks into a busy Blackpool police station. Through a crowd of people waiting to be seen or those brought in after arrest, she is recognised by Detective Harry Carter, who is at the desk after bringing in a pick pocket. He hands him to a nearby constable to deal with and walks over to greet her.

'Miss May. What can we do for you?'

It's clear the train journey from Liverpool has been drenched in tears. Katherine's eyes appearing red sore and dog tired. This woman looks like she has not slept for years. 'Detective Carter. I need to speak to you. I have been going mad at home over what has happened.'

He smiles. 'Miss May would you care to accompany me down the prom?' Katherine dries her eyes whilst nodding. 'That would be lovely Detective Carter.' He lifts his arm so she can link him and they leave the station.

Watched as they go by Chief Inspector Sydney Appleton.

He appears worried. Katherine May's appearance is something Appleton doesn't need. He has convinced himself that her son is going to escape punishment for his crimes and this sickens him to the heart.

The small matter of a war on and Blackpool swiftly descending into Dodge City by the sea keeps him occupied.

But in quieter moments,

when lying in bed or staring at the bottom of a glass, it hurts; a burning anger of resentment is eating this Blackpool copper up from the inside.

'Be careful Harry' he says quietly to himself, as the two disappear around a corner.

'Watch your back son.'

Carter and Katherine are dodging the crowds walking down the North pier. It is early afternoon and hundreds are milling around. Organ music resonates loud and the smell of alcohol sifts through the air. There is a heady concoction of uniforms and party people trying just that little too hard to let their hair down one last time. A sense of coming doom amidst the forced laughter echoing as a constant ghastly reminder that the Germans are on the way.

They come to a multi-coloured booth emblazoned in stars and the words. *Madame Marie's.* On its wall a poster claims...*Let the Gypsy lady tell your fortune...*

Katherine turns to Carter. 'I want to go in. Come on.'

She grabs his hand and they enter. Awaiting them is a black veiled lady sat at a table with a crystal ball in front of her. She has rings on every finger and speaks with a soft Irish accent.

'Put your half a crown in the box on this table lovely and I will tell your pretty lady here what the stars have in store for her.'

Madame Marie motions for them both to sit. Through her veil she eyes Katherine, who suddenly clutches hold of Carter's hand tight. He can feel her shaking with nerves. 'We don't have to do this?' He says.

'No I want to' replies a smiling Katherine. 'It's just a bit of fun.'

But one look at her face makes Carter think this could go horribly wrong.

Madame Marie coughs loud as if to insinuate she is ready to begin.

Wearing black velvet gloves the gypsy places both hands on the crystal ball and gazes deep into it.

Katherine takes a deep breath.

'A picture is forming. I see a young man many years ago. In the distance there are ships in a harbour. He is not from these shores.'

Her face appears puzzled. 'I recognise him from somewhere.'

Katherine squeezes even tighter Carter's hand.

'There is a pretty young girl by his side. They are holding hands and clearly in love.' Madame Marie looks up at Katherine and smiles.

'I believe it is you dear.'

She continues. 'This picture is now fading and another is forming. I see a young boy, no more than ten. He is stood looking out over the ocean. He is lonely. It is like he is waiting for someone to return. He is the son of the first man. Whom I take is your husband?'

Katherine says nothing but her look gives all away.

'I see' say Madame Marie. 'He is no longer around. This is now also fading but there will be one more for your half a crown.

The most is clearing.' Suddenly Madame Marie starts to scream!

Carter pulls Katherine up and drags her to the door.

Katherine can't take her eyes off the gypsy lady.

'What do you see?' She pleads. 'Please tell me what you see?'

Madame Marie removes her veil and has tears streaming down her face.

'You gave birth to a monster. Now get out!'

'Tell me what you see?' Cries Katherine. 'Please?'
Carter places an arm around Katherine's shoulder and tries
to push her through the door.

'You want to know what I saw?' Shouts the Gypsy.
Katherine nods.

'I saw your boy and Adolf Hitler embracing like father
and son. And I saw rivers of blood on this beach. I saw the
faces of three innocent girls looking back at me. And I
know who killed them. Now I don't want to know or
understand anymore, so you get out of her now. Go on
leave!'

Carter grabs Katherine and pulls her by the arm back
outside onto the pier.

Inside the sound of Madame Marie sobbing loud can be
heard.

A hysterical Katherine won't be calmed.

'I let one murdering freak sleep with me and gave birth to
his monster Mr Carter. Can you imagine how that feels?
What my own flesh and blood has done to those girls.'

'You're not to blame Katherine. In no way is it your fault.
None of us can help who we fall in love with. Or how our
kids are going to turn out. Life is a toss of a coin. If it falls
one way then all is sweetness and light. But if it drops in
the gutter? Then the path can be dark and troubled. There
is no rhyme or reason to life. It's just life.'

Around them people are staring across.

Katherine notices this. 'I want to go home Mr Carter. It
was a mistake coming here today. I just felt like it was
something I had to do. Will you take me back to Liverpool
now please?'

Carter smiles. 'Of course I will. He puts an arm around
her shoulders.

'Come on let's get out of here.'

Later that night Chief Inspector Appleton is still in his office working. It has gone eleven o'clock and between endless paperwork, he is slowly working himself through a bottle of whiskey. An unexpected knock at the door brings in a young unformed constable. Twenty one year old, local boy, Bobby Baines. Normally smiling and full of life, this time he appears close to tears, his face is drained of any colour.

'Bobby what the hell is up? You look bloody awful son.'
Boss I've got some bad news. We've just had a phone call from the Liverpool boys. There's been a terrible accident.'
'What kind of accident? What are you talking about?'
'It's Detective Carter and Katherine May.'
'What about them?' Asks an increasingly frustrated Appleton.
They're dead. Both were killed earlier tonight when Detective Carter's car tried to run an army blockade outside Liverpool.'
Baines has tears falling down his cheeks. 'I'm so sorry boss.'
Appleton is struggling to take this in. He stands and goes towards Baines who is clearly heartbroken. Appleton puts an arm around him.
He ushers Baines to sit down and pours him a glass full of whiskey.
'Drink this in one go lad.'
The constable does so
'Now from the beginning, tell me all you know?'
'Baines puts down his glass. 'It was an Inspector Mackenzie from the Merseyside police. They had been informed by an army officer who walked in off the street. He said that Detective Carter and the May woman had

been drinking. And that after two warnings they refused all attempt to stops and so the army opened fire. The military have the bodies at an army camp in Kirby.'

'This is utter madness' exclaims Appleton.

'There's not a chance in hell Harry would pull this kind of stunt. It simply doesn't add up. Somebody somewhere is covering their fuckin' tracks. First thing in the morning Bobby, I'm going over to that camp. Now go on and get yourself cleaned up before going back on the duty desk.'

Baines stands 'Did Detective Carter have any family boss?'

Appleton sighs. 'No one, his mum died two years ago. There was nobody else…..Except me.' The inspector is struggling to hold it together.

'Go on get going lad.'

Baines leaves the office.

A devastated Appleton collapses back on his chair. Utterly convinced that Carter and Katherine have been purposely killed to silence them. He takes out a revolver from the draw and puts it in a jacket pocket hanging over the chair.

AT ANY PRICE

It is a drunken Inspector Appleton who staggers into Paddy Owen's Empire Ballroom bar, just short of midnight. It has been raining heavily and Appleton's coat and hat are soaked to the skin. He still has a small bottle of whiskey in his hand. It is half full as Appleton takes another gulp.

He looks around the packed room and catches Paddy Owen's eye.

The owner smiles and walks across to the Inspector. 'Are you okay Sydney? You looked shocking mate.'

'I need to speak to you Pat, but not in here. Somewhere private.'

Appleton is staggering. Owen takes his arm.

'Come with me Detective, we can't have Blackpool's finest policeman falling over in front of this evil lot.'

Owen leads Appleton out of the bar. They head up a long winding staircase.

'Where are we fuckin' going Paddy?

Owen laughs. 'You said you wanted privacy. I'm taking you to my eagle's nest.'

They finally reach the top floor.

'You're going to love this' says Owen. He shows Appleton into a sparse room with a huge wide reaching window that has a panoramic views of Blackpool's prom.

Owen pulls up two comfy chairs by the glass, then goes in a fridge and pulls out a large bottle of whiskey.

'Ireland's finest my friend. Put that rubbish away your drinking and we'll share this.'

Owen starts to pour when Appleton's words cut him like a thunder bolt.

Harry is dead Pat.'

He looks up. 'What did you just say?'

'Harry is dead. It happened this afternoon at an army roadblock outside Liverpool. He was taking Freddie May's mother, Katherine home. She was killed as well. The army have given me a cock and bull story that Harry tried to run the roadblock, but that is fuckin' nonsense. They have seen him off. Shut him up permanently'

A shocked Owen hands Appleton a drink and sits down. Clearly struggling to come to terms with what he's listening to.

'Syd I don't understand? What reason would anyone have to murder Harry? Especially the authorities. I mean, he's a copper for God's sakes. One of your lot. A good guy.'

Appleton smiles and drinks his whiskey in one go. 'If you are sitting comfortable Pat I'm going to tell you a wild fuckin' story....'

Ten minutes later Appleton finishes and Owen sits stunned and shaken.

'Adolf Hitler? My God Syd, what have you got yourself mixed up in?

And you're convinced they killed Harry and the May woman?'

Harry nods. 'Every bone in my body is telling me it wasn't just a trigger happy squaddie. I'm a copper and none of this smells right.'

Well the stakes have never been higher' replies Owen.

'I'll grant you that. But I still find it hard to believe our own side are capable of stooping so low.'

C'mon Pat, you're not naïve. We're at war and losing and standing on the edge of being invaded. Bloody hell our grandkids are going to be talking fuckin' German. In these circumstances the lives of a Blackpool copper and a woman nobody has heard of from Liverpool, I hate to say it, are hardly important. And are never going to register to anybody. Except me.

These people can do what they want, to who they want. There's no law anymore, at any price. No right or wrong. Just a survival instinct which blurs peoples consciences and takes away any pangs of guilt.'

'What do you think they are planning to do with May?

'Who knows' replies Appleton. Shrugging his shoulders and refilling their glasses. 'I'm only telling you this old pal, because if anything happens to me. If you hear a fairytale that I blew my own brains out. Or got hit by a car. Or even fell off the top of Blackpool fuckin' tower. Then at least someone will know that it isn't my style to be so clumsy.'

'So what are you planning to do?' Asks a still stunned Owen.

'Tomorrow I'm going to the army base to identify Harry and Katherine's bodies. But first port of call is the Liverpool police station where their deaths were reported. I'm going to snoop around. See what comes up.'

Paddy raises his glass. 'To Harry.' Appleton does similar and they chink glasses.

'I'll do some asking around myself says Owen. You never know what might pop up. If I hear anything I'll let you know.'

Appleton nods. 'Crazy times.'

Both men look out the wide framed windows as a ferocious storm from the Irish Sea sweeps down upon

Blackpool's prom. The waves rising and crashing against the shore. Above thunder cracks and a lightning bolt strikes the tower.

'Jesus Syd' says Owen. As they watch in shock as it appears to glow, shimmer and even momentarily rock.

If this is what the end of the world feels like, then I think we should finish this bottle and start another.'

Toxteth Police Station: Late next morning a hungover, grim faced Inspector Sydney Appleton walks up to the reception desk. Behind it stands forty six year old Sergeant Bill Ross. Large, no nonsense man with old school ideas. He stares at Appleton. Clearly aware he is the worse for wear.

'What can we do for you sir?'

Appleton shows Ross his ID. 'I'm Inspector Appleton from Blackpool police. One of my men was killed yesterday by the army just a few miles from here. Along with a lady. Katherine May from this area. I'd like to ask Inspector Mackenzie a few questions before I go and identify their bodies over at Kirby Military base.'

Ross steps out from behind the desk. 'If you'll follow me.'

He leads Appleton down a small corridor before stopping and pointing at a door. Ross knocks and opens it.

Forty year old Inspector Henry Mackenzie is sat at his desk. A balding man, tall with haunted eyes and a tired drawn face.

'Sir this is Inspector Appleton from Blackpool police. He would like a quick word.'

Ross leaves as Mackenzie stands and shakes Appleton's hand.

'First I would like to say how sorry I am for the loss of Detective Collins. I heard he was a good man and a top class copper. Bloody soldiers. Kids mostly scared of their own shadows. They see German paratroopers behind every fuckin' wall and tree. Tragic.'

'This officer who reported the incident' asks Appleton. 'What was he like?'

Mackenzie shrugs his shoulders. 'A strange bloke really. Stiff upper lipped, your Eton type. A Captain in rank. By the name of Mallory. I did notice one particular scar under his right eye. Looked like it had been done by a razor.

I see a lot them around there. Also?'

'Go on' urges Appleton

'Well his uniform insignia was that of the Royal Fusiliers. But he claimed to be of the Grenadier guards who are stationed over at Kirby. A point picked up by Sergeant Ross out there. Himself a former Grenadier. Really not something you would expect from an officer and alleged gentleman don't you think?'

Appleton appears deep in thought. He looks Mackenzie straight in the eyes.

'I think this man you met was military intelligence and I also believe that my boy and the woman were killed purposely. By who exactly? Well I intend to find out.'

'A shocked Mackenzie sits back down at his desk, 'Inspector Appleton, I think you're upset and clearly not thinking straight. Why on earth would the British army have reason to execute a serving policeman and an innocent woman?'

'I know it must sound like the rantings of a madman Mackenzie, but I have my reasons for thinking such. I really can't explain any further. It's for your own good and you wouldn't believe me anyway.'

'Well I can promise you Inspector Appleton, this conversation doesn't leave these four walls. I've never met you, but I know of your reputation on the force and from our little chat here it's clear to me you're not mad. Misguided maybe, now I'm not saying I believe you, but for peace of mind I would like Sergeant Ross to accompany you to the camp.
 If that's okay with you?'
Appleton nods. 'Thanks I appreciate it.'
Mackenzie smiles. 'The sergeant is a good man. If there's something rotten going on he'll sense it. Old school is our Bill. Once in never out.'

Military Base Kirby: The car carrying Inspector Appleton and Sergeant Ross pulls up at the gates of the camp. A young soldier with a rifle hoisted over his shoulder approaches them. Watched from nearby by four others. All staring intently towards the visitors.
 A feeling of tension cuts through the air. Appleton is driving and Ross is next to him. He can feel the nerves. 'Something is bothering this lot' he mutters quietly under his breath. The soldiers urges Appleton to wind open the window. He does so.
'Your business here today sir?'
 Appleton hand over his ID. 'I'm here to identify the body of my colleague Harry Carter and the woman Katherine May.
 Ross passes his over also and after a momentarily glance the soldier hands them both back.
 'Please go through.' He motions for the barrier to be opened.
'Thank you' replies Appleton. I'm looking for a Captain Mallory?'

The soldier appears quizzical. 'We've no one of that name here sir. You must be mistaken.' He points inside the camp.

'The third building on the right is the officer's mess. If you present yourself there then I'm sure somebody will sort you out.'

'Cheers son' replies Appleton. Whilst winding down the window.

'There's no mistake Inspector' says Ross. 'The bastard called himself Mallory.'

' I know Sergeant' he replies. 'I believe you. Let's go see what they have to say for themselves.'

It's a small hut kitted out at various spots with tables and chairs. A man made wooden bar serving around a dozen officers relaxing, reading chatting and drinking. Appleton and Ross enter. All eyes fall upon them. A voice with tones of Eton echoes loud in their direction.

'Who the bloody hell are you?' A tall man, a Lieutenant, slim with unsmiling features and a thin dander moustache approaches.

'How dare you come in here without knocking? Damn civilians.'

Appleton shows him his police ID. 'This entitles me to go where I want. Now I'm here to identify the bodies.'

He looks around the room at the faces glaring back. 'Can one of you fine gentlemen please show me and my colleague here the way? Then afterwards I would like to ask a few questions on yesterday's events. Starting with who and where the fuck is Captain Mallory?'

A voice from behind suddenly startles. 'I think you'll find that's me.'

Appleton and Ross turn around and stood facing them is a black-suited. thirty one year old MI6 agent, Captain Tim Mallory. A slender figure with blond hair, a seemingly pleasant handsome face, but with a scar, zig-zagging under his right eye. Eyes that undoubtedly hide a thousand dark secrets.

Mallory smiles 'What can I do for you gentlemen?' He speaks with a soft upper crust brogue.

'I see you got rid of the uniform?' Replies Ross.

'You don't question me Sergeant. Now if you'll both follow me I'll take you to the bodies.'

He goes to walk off, only for Appleton to call after him.

'Just a minute Mallory I want a word with you?'

He stops and turns around. 'Captain Mallory to you Inspector Appleton.'

How do you know my name?'

'Mallory takes out a pack of cigarette from his jacket pocket and lights one with a silver lighter. He inhales then smiles. 'Are you fucking serious?'

'Oh I get it' replies Appleton. 'I suppose I'm next on your list? What will it be for me then? Found dead in the bath. A suicide verdict. Or are you just going to throw me out of a tenth floor fuckin' window.'

Sergeant Ross looks on dumfounded, whilst Mallory hardly flutters an eyebrow. 'I have absolutely no idea what you are ranting on about Inspector. I would calm down if I was you, before you say something you might regret.'

'Who the hell are you Mallory?'

Who am I? I am your God, Chief Inspector Appleton. I am your children's Father Christmas and your wife's secret lover. I am an angel of death wearing a white robe, a false fucking halo and a bible stamped *Facere Valint.* Do you know your Latin? It means *'Do whatever.'* And without emotion or mercy to keep these Nazi vermin from our shores. Because if they come, then day becomes night and the dark becomes hell on this earth. I and people like me are your last hope. I am a wolf in sheep's clothing. I am a hidden dagger. I am the sniper's bullet you don't see coming. I am your brother in arms Inspector Appleton. And I reside so high in rank above you it is hard to fucking breathe up here. Now have I answered your question?'

Appleton appears stunned. Without saying it, Mallory, in the Inspector's eyes, has just admitted to killing Harry Carter and Katherine May.

Mallory recognises as much in Appleton's eyes.

'They tried to run the roadblock Inspector. Your man panicked and I gave the order to open fire. Now Carter was found with a revolver on his person. My actions to execute an armed response were more than justifiable under these circumstances.'

Sergeant Ross interrupts. 'I've heard enough. What kind of circumstances allows you to gun down a police officer and an unarmed woman? We are talking about the law of the land here? I'm afraid you're going to have to accompany me back to the station Captain Mallory.'

'I don't think so Sergeant. Mallory hands him over a piece of paper.

Ross reads then passes it to Appleton, who speaks out loud.

'This order gives Captain Timothy Mallory full freedom to act on my behalf and to answer to nobody but myself. Prime Minister: Winston S Churchill.'

Appleton gives it back to Mallory. 'So these measly words give you licence to kill my men and innocent bystanders?'

Suddenly four soldiers arrive on the scene. Their rifles unholstered and eyes focused upon Appleton and Ross.

Captain Mallory addresses one in particular. A young corporal. Twenty one year old Charlie Hickson. Tough features, a pre-war boxer. A Scouser, stocky and well built. 'Corporal Hickson, you will accompany these two men to the open coffins over at the temporary morgue. Once a positive identification has been established, escort them back to their car and off the camp. Is that understood?' Hickson snaps to attention. 'Yes Sir!'

Mallory faces the policemen. 'So long gentlemen we won't ever meet again. I'm sure you'll be glad to know.'

Appleton explodes in anger. 'I'm not letting you get away with this Mallory. I believe it was cold bloodied murder. No matter how long it takes I'll ensure justice will be done and no note from Churchill will save you. Why? Give me one reason why Harry and the May woman had to be killed. It makes no sense.

'As I have already stated Inspector, they tried to run the road...'

'What exactly was the roadblock up for?' Interrupts Ross. Mallory smiles. 'Well it was to keep your people in Sergeant. You see we can't have civilians leaving the city. It wouldn't look good. Bad for morale.'

Ross can't believe his ears. 'Those poor bastards are being bombed to hell and you send them back?'

'Terrible I know but we can't have panic. Now run along with Corporal Hickson, here, there's a good fucking chap.' The four soldiers crowd around the policemen.

'We will meet again Mallory' calls out Appleton. 'I promise you.'

'Have a safe journey back to Blackpool Inspector Appleton,' he replies.

Whilst starting to light up another cigarette. 'I hear it's quite lively at the moment.'

They are led away.

'Oh and one last thing Inspector' shouts Mallory.

Appleton looks around.

Mallory is smiling wide. 'Did you know your Detective Carter was a Nancy boy? That's right a poof. His name was mentioned by a young soldier currently in a military detention centre in Lytham. A young Irish fairy by the name of Rafferty. You really should vet your men better Chief Inspector.

Doesn't look good on you. They start terrible rumours these kinds of things. Makes our boys easy blackmail targets for German spies. Are you married yourself?'

Appleton simply stares and says nothing. The fact he is and has four children is not something Appleton wishes to share with this man, whom he would love nothing better than to strangle.

Instead Appleton turns and walks away.

The policemen and their armed escort enter a small wooden hut. Empty, a shell, apart from two open coffins in its centre.

Corporal Hickson puts a hand on Inspector Appleton's arm. 'Sir would you like to follow me.' They head across. Appleton removes his hat. A face solemn and near to tears, he stares down at Harry Carter's face. The features scarred and cut up.

We did our best to clean him up' whispers Hickson. 'But there was a lot of damage. Can you confirm this is Detective Carter sir?'

Appleton nods, then glances over at the other corpse.

'And this lady, Corporal, is Katherine May.'

'Thank you Inspector' replies Hickson.

'Would you like some time alone. We can wait outside?'
Appleton looks across at Ross and the other three soldiers.
He turns to Hickson. 'I would like a minute alone with you
if you don't mind son?'

'Of course.' Hickson nods over to his men and they and
Ross step outside, leaving the two men stood by the
coffins.

'Were you present Corporal?'

'I was.'

'Well then tell me what happened to my officer and this
lady yesterday?'

'I'm not at liberty to talk about it sir.'

'Oh don't give me that fuckin' crap!' Snaps an angry
Appleton. '

'I can tell you're a good lad. A good soldier. Honest and
decent. Liverpool stock. You know the difference between
right and wrong. Now I'll ask you again. What happened
yesterday? I just need a one word answer. Was it right or
wrong?'

   Hickson looks towards the door. He appears nervous.

'It was wrong sir. The order was given to fire and when a
Captain issues such there is no option. There's a fuckin'
war on. We just assumed a German spy was in the car.'

   'And was it slowing down coming towards you?'

Hickson nods. 'I remember looking over towards Captain
Mallory. He appeared to recognise who was in it and gave
the order to fire. Christ they never had a chance. There
were two tommy guns and six rifles aimed on them.'

   Hickson looks down at Carter's body. 'I'm really sorry
Inspector.'

'What happened then?' Asks Appleton.

'Well Mallory went over to the car and found a revolver on your man's body.'

'I gave Harry that gun to protect himself. A lot of good that did him'

Hickson appears ashen faced and sick to the stomach.

'Inspector, afterwards I approached Captain Mallory and asked him who it was we had killed? He dismissed me and said that it was a matter of national security. He told me I could be executed if I discussed this with anyone, so I would appreciate if you kept this conversation to yourself.'

Appleton smiles. 'No problem Corporal.'

He puts his hand out and Hickson accepts it.

'Good luck in the coming months soldier. You keep your head down.'

'I survived Dunkirk Inspector' smiles Hickson. 'Nothing could ever be worse than that. And the top brass made it out to be a glorious victory? We were chased off the fuckin' beach for God's sake. I have men here on this camp that haven't got rifles. What are we going to do if German paratroopers drop, throw fuckin' apples at them?'

'Well you're still here to tell the story son and to fight another day. So long.'

'You too' replies Hickson.

'Take care of yourself.'

Inspector Appleton and Sergeant Ross are in the car heading back to Toxteth Police Station. Ross's head is spinning at all that has just occurred.

'I'm not even going to ask what has just gone on Inspector.'

'Well that's fine Sergeant' replies a smiling Appleton. 'Because I'm not going to tell you. Please believe me when I say it's for your own good.

But thanks for today.'
Ross appears perplexed. 'What exactly did I do?'
'You did the right thing Sergeant Ross' replies Appleton.
'A rare occurrence these days.'

JOUSTING WITH THE SEA WOLF

The English Channel. It is well past midnight and a nervous looking Major James Willard stands alone on board the deck of the destroyer *HMS Manchester*. The sea is calm, whilst above a full moon shines bright and a plethora of stars illuminate the stilled waters of the English Channel. They are close to the agreed meeting position. A halfway point where a German U Boat will surface and for five minutes only hostilities will cease whilst Willard boards the enemy vessel. From there the short journey back to German-occupied France, then by plane to Germany and a meeting with the Fuhrer Adolf Hitler, to inform him of Churchill's proposition. One so utterly outrageous, Willard thinks his Prime Minister is mad to even attempt it. But such is their precarious position, anything, no matter how absurd or desperate is deemed worth a try, when the alternative is Nazi enslavery.

Behind Willard, Captain Charles Scott. A large impressive figure. Splendid in his Royal Navy white uniform appears.

'You appear a little worried Major' says Scott.

'Absolutely no need to be. We've just made contact with the U Boat and they have confirmed everything is right on schedule. All a little bloody surreal if you ask me?'

'It certainly is Captain Scott' replies a smiling Willard. 'I appreciate your help in this matter and can assure you it's no less strange for me.'

'Quite Major. Well I can only wish you luck in your mission.'

He offers Willard his hand and the two men shake.

'Thank you Captain. I believe I'm going to need it.'
Suddenly a voice shouts loud from above them.
 'Captain, 200 degree starboard bow. She's surfacing!'
 The two men look out and indeed the outline of a
submarine is clear in the moonlight. A figure is seen
putting up a white flag. Willard smiles.
'Well then, I suppose I best brush up on my German.'
   A small dinghy is launched to take Major Willard over
the short distance to the U Boat. Awaiting him and giving
Willard a helping hand to climb up are two German
submariners. Both huge men. Bearded and smiling towards
Willard.
 'Come Englishman' says one, hoisting him aboard.
 'Our Captain is waiting for you in his cabin.'
 The other takes down the white flag and waves across at
the British destroyer. He gives it a two fingered salute and
the three men disappear inside the U Boat. Watching all
this through binoculars is Captain Scott. His mind is racing
to the possibilities of Willard's mission.
   Finally the submarine disappears back beneath the water.
Scott puts down his binoculars. He speaks quietly to
himself.
'The one time we have one at our mercy and the bastards
are under a white flag. Good luck Major Willard. This
better be worth it.'

   Sandwiched between the two submariners who brought
him aboard, Willard is led down through the U Boat.
Every eye on board appears to be on him. Who is this
Englishman? What is he doing here. Looks of incredulity
are on their faces.

'What's up with you?' Shouts one of Willard's entourage. 'Have you never seen a real life fucking Englishman before?'

 'Not a live one!' Comes the reply.

 They all laugh. Willard hears this, his German good enough to understand the comments. They unnerve him a little.

 Finally they arrive outside a small room.

'Our Captain awaits you Sir. Please go in.'

Willard enters.

 Stood waiting to greet him is the German navy's most successful and decorated officer. Thirty four year old Captain Pieter Hessler. A tall bearded figure. A man who clearly commands respect from his crew. Haunting, engaging eyes, with a quick smile. Hessler is no Nazi, but this holder of the Iron Cross has not earned the nickname of the Sea Wolf for nothing. His cunning, bravery and unerring ability to destroy and then disappear has seen him sink thousands of British tonnage. And today Hessler stands staring at Major James Willard, with absolutely no idea why this Englishman dressed in a businessman's suit is aboard his boat.

 Willard salutes. 'Major James Willard.'

 Hessler returns this, but it is a half-hearted effort.

 'Captain Pieter Hessler, Major. Can I interest you in a brandy?'

'Yes please' replies Willard. 'My stomach is rather churning First time on a submarine. Especially a German one.'

 Hessler smiles. 'They are all basically the same.'

He pours two large brandies from a bottle into mugs and passes one to Willard. Hessler raises his drink.

 'To a successful venture Major'

Willard does similar and the men toast.

'To a better world Captain Hessler.'

Off course' replies Hessler. 'Fine words. You English. You always seem to find the correct expression to suit the occasion. Obviously the result of a fine and expensive education Major Willard. I would say Cambridge?'

'Yes Captain. How on earth did you guess?'

'I myself spent time there. You have that look and may I be so bold as to say, the way you hold yourself. A true gentleman sir. Welcome aboard U Boat 235.'

'You was educated at Cambridge?'

'I was. Unfortunately due to my father's untimely death I was forced to return home and look after the family business.'

'I am sorry' replies Willard. 'What business was this?'

'Can you believe looking at this tramp before you that Hessler's was one of the most renowned clothing firms for gentlemen across Europe. Indeed some of our best customers were based in England. Including your Royal family. Lovely people, if a little, may I say away with the fairies.'

Willard laughs. 'I was never fortunate or important enough to mix in their company Captain Hessler. I will have to take your word on that particular matter. I couldn't possibly comment. Rather ironic that once you dressed them, now you sink their ships. I hope they paid in advance. Rather think if not you may not now get your money.'

'Ah you English' replies Hessler. 'One of the many things I miss about living in your country. The ability to insult without even trying. It is a wonderful talent.'

'We are who we are Captain' replies Willard. 'As I'm sure you'll become quickly aware of if you try visiting again any time soon.'

Hessler smiles. 'I take no pleasure in this war Major. We are merely pawns in a much larger game. One I sincerely hope with whatever your reasons for being here can shorten.'

Willard takes another large gulp of his brandy.
'So do I Captain. Forgive me, but from what you've said, can I presume you're no dyed in the wool, fanatical Nazi?'
'You presume correct. But that doesn't deter me from ensuring when the opportunity arises that I don't do my duty and try to sink anything sailing with a Union Jack insignia flying.'

'I suppose in war we both rage at opposing colours?'
'Indeed' replies Hessler. 'It has always been so. But I also believe the rules of war as written allow that between the shooting, we can act like civilised human beings. We after all did not start the fire Major Willard. As soldiers have claimed for hundreds of years, we are now simply following orders?'

'The oldest excuse in the book I fear,' sighs Willard.
'Please sit' says Hessler. They both pull up chairs at a small table.
The captain refills their mugs.

'To warm you on your journey to Berlin Major Willard.'
Hessler smiles. 'My orders are to drop you at Calais, from there a plane will take you to Germany. Can I ask you something? We do not have much time together and there is something that deeply puzzles me.'
'If I can answer Captain. Of course. Ask away.'

'Why does Churchill continue to insist on fighting on? Surely you know your cause is hopeless. In a short time the opportunity for a negotiated peace will pass and the British people will be subjected to all the excesses of the Nazis.'

'You talk Captain as if you should be on our side.'

'I talk as a German, Major Willard. I fight for my country. Those boys you saw coming in here are my responsibility. It is my job to keep them alive. The politics of this ghastly mess is not something I associated myself with.'

Willard smiles. 'The answer to your question. We will fight on Captain Hessler. For we have no choice. It is inherent in the genes you see. The British despite our image abroad for cricket and afternoon tea have always been a warlike race. We love a good scrap whatever the odds.

Remember Napoleon? Another empire builder, a small man with illusions of grandeur. Similar to your little Corporal in Berlin. He made the mistake of underestimating us and paid the price. You watch, you just damn well watch. We will surprise you and somehow, although it may be a long and bloody struggle. The British people will prevail.'

'Again excellent words Major. But sadly a requiem for the damned. For it is not based on reality. Each day I'm putting more of your ships at the bottom of the channel. It is becoming a graveyard for your men. I have seen with my own eyes what is set to be waged against your towns and cities.'

'Well so far our boys in the RAF are more than holding their own. I don't know what you're being told Captain Hessler, but we are knocking Luftwaffe bombers out of the sky at a rate of four to one. This war is far from won. If you don't win the battle of skies then we will destroy anything you send over the channel.'

Willard notices a miniature wolf's head pinned on Hessler's black leather jacket.

'Is that a good luck charm?'

An embarrassed Hessler laughs. 'No, it was a birthday gift off the men. I have been given the rather absurd nickname of the Sea Wolf.'

'I think it suits you Captain Hessler. And I must say. I have rather enjoyed my verbal jousting with the Sea Wolf.'

BODY OF CHRIST

Inspector Sydney Appleton is sat in his office when there is a knock at the door Flight Lieutenant Jan Zumbach enters.

'Inspector I heard the news about Harry and Katherine May. On behalf of my General and all of us I would like to extend our deepest condolences.'

Appleton smiles. 'Come in Lieutenant, take a seat.'

Zumbach does so. 'What did the army say?'

'They claimed Harry tried to run a roadblock and they had no option but to fire. I don't believe a word of it.'

'I don't understand?'

'Look' replies Appleton. 'I need to go and speak to someone banged up in the military glasshouse in Lytham. If you tag along young man I'll tell you a story. It's one you'll find hard to believe, but it's all true. Okay?'

A confused Zumbach nods. 'Of course yes.'

And so on the way to visit Corporal George Rafferty to ask about his relationship with Harry Carter, Inspector Appleton fills in Zumbach with all that has occurred.

He listens on in stunned silence.

Finally Zumbach manages to speak. 'I didn't know Harry for long, but found him a good and decent man. Anything you need Inspector, I'm here to help.'

These words don't surprise Appleton. He recognises the same quality in Zumbach possessed by Harry Carter. What Carter did in his private life, whilst shocking him, changes nothing of the Inspector's deep regard for his young colleague. He is missing him, and feels a sense of duty to do justice to Carter's memory. He did not deserve to die in those circumstances. Gunned down in a hail of machine gun bullets like a thirties Chicago gangster.

'Thank you Lieutenant. I appreciate your words. I want to find out off Rafferty just how Harry's name came up in his case. And when and to who. Something tells me my mysterious spook Captain friend may well pop up in the conversation.'

A red capped military MP unlocks George Rafferty's cell, who is lying on his bunk staring at the ceiling. 'Get up Rafferty you lazy Irish bastard!' Shouts the MP in his direction. 'You've got company. This here is Inspector Appleton. He would like a word with you.'

Slowly Rafferty rises.
He looks over towards Appleton and Zumbach. His face swollen, eyes blackened and lip busted.

'What happened to you Corporal?' Asks Appleton. Rafferty smiles ruefully. 'I slipped Inspector.'

I'm sure you did. Sit down son.' Appleton stares at the MP who won't meet his eyes. Instead he leaves the cell. From outside he yells back. 'You've ten minutes.'

Appleton waits till he has disappeared then begins. 'So then. Tell me who you mentioned Harry Carter's name to?'

'Have you got a cigarette? 'Asks Rafferty.
Zumbach takes out a packet and hands him one over. Appleton lights it for him.

'Thank you Inspector. They told me about what happened to Harry. I'm really sorry.'
'Who told you?'

'An army Captain. He turned up shortly after I was arrested. The MP's told me when charged, that if I mentioned names I had been involved with, then it would be a little easier on me. So I did so, it's not something I'm proud of.

I really liked Harry. But I don't want to be stuck in a fuckin' jail cell when the Krauts arrive. Wearing a uniform will I'm sure be enough for a death sentence, but if they find out what I'm in here for?'

'This Captain' asks Appleton. 'What did he look like?'

'Strange really. A gentleman type, but a real hard bastard. He had a scar under his right eye.'

Appleton's eyes look to the cell roof. 'His name is Mallory Corporal. And he's no Captain. What did he want to know about Detective Carter?'

'Where I met him. If I had slept with any other coppers?'

'As a matter of interest' asks Appleton. 'Where did you meet Harry?'

'Seadogs.'

'Jesus' he exclaims. 'That den of iniquity.'

'What is Seadogs?' Asks Zumbach.

'I doubt you Poles will have a word for it. But imagine a freak circus with a bar.'

'I'm no freak Inspector' snaps Rafferty. 'And neither was Harry Carter. I don't remember anyone calling me that when I was at Dunkirk. One of the last off the beach. We were part of the rearguard and it was a miracle any of us made it home. Funny how a man can be classed a hero one minute, and then because he doesn't fit in with the rest when the bullets have stopped firing, suddenly become a freak?

Locking me in this cell because I prefer apples when most men like oranges. We can't all be the same Inspector Appleton. The fact I wasn't born with your tastes and prefer what the bible call forbidden fruit, does that make me any less of a man? Or a soldier? My blood will bleed fuckin' red when the time comes.

Like yours or your friend here. Or even the body of Christ in that damn book.

So fuck you with your freak show.

And the British army. Now if you don't mind I'm not going to speak anymore. Apart from to say Harry was a good man.

And I'm sure he was a decent copper as well.'

Inspector Appleton and Lieutenant Zumbach have stood and listened. Both are clearly numbed by Corporal Rafferty's outburst.

Finally Zumbach hands his cigarette and matches to Rafferty.

'Good luck Corporal' says Appleton.

'I'm not judging you and the freak line was out of order. Harry was like a son to me. And I promise you I won't stop until he gets justice.'

Both men head off out of the cell, only for Rafferty to call after them.

'Inspector.'

Appleton turns around.

'This Mallory. He came across more of a Nazi than the ones we are fighting. Surely if we can't tell the difference anymore then this war is a waste of fuckin' time?'

Appleton and Zumbach are walking back to the car. Both men are quiet. Finally Appleton breaks the silence. 'Well it's clear Rafferty knows nothing about what's going on, so he should be safe enough.'

'What do we do now?' Asks Zumbach.

'There's no we Lieutenant. The reason I informed you what's really going on here is because I believe your life could well be in danger. This mad bastard Mallory will stop at nothing to ensure the story never gets out. That will include if the chance arises getting rid of me, and if he can, you as well.

So my advice is watch your back. Stay amongst your own people and if anyone contacts you ring me immediately. Is that understood?'

Zumbach nods. 'And what are you going to do?'

'Me' smiles Appleton. 'I'm going to do my job Lieutenant. I'm going to be a policeman and uphold the law.'

LIKE FATHER LIKE SON

Germany. It is a miserable rainy, cold, mid-morning when the Junker transport plane escorted by a pair of Messerschmitt fighters lands in Berlin. With two Abwehr intelligence officers alongside him, Major James Willard, carrying a small brief case is led off the aircraft.

Stood waiting to greet him is a smiling Admiral Canaris.

The two men salute and shake hands. Willard knows who this man is by surveillance photographs.

'My name is Major James Willard. I'm sure you're as bemused by all this as I am Admiral?'

'Oh you know me? Forgive my ignorance for not knowing you Major.'

'Oh that's quite alright. I am nowhere near as important as the head of German Intelligence.'

Canaris smiles. 'Quite, but I'm sure you are man of some standing.

Otherwise you would not be here today. And let us hope from this madness something good may emerge?'

'On that we can definitely both agree Sir,' replies Willard

'Come Major.' Canaris leads the Englishman to a waiting car.

'The Fuhrer is eagerly anticipating your arrival.'

Willard smiles warily. 'I'm sure he is Admiral. I cannot say the feeling is mutual.'

'Let me assure you Major Willard. No harm will befall you whilst here in Berlin. Not only are you under a flag of truce, but you have my word as a Germany officer on this matter.'

'Thank you Admiral' replies Willard. Fully appreciating Canaris' words, but still not sure it will make any difference when Hitler sees what he is carrying in the briefcase.

Reich Chancellery: Adolf Hitler is alone in the private quarters. He is pacing furiously with hands behind his back. Fully aware that the Englishman has landed and is being at this very moment brought before him. Inside Hitler seethes with blind fury and wild curiosity.

The name of the woman Katherine May has been blotted from his brain for so long. Put away in a small vault inside the head. Never again to emerge and safe in the knowledge that no one will ever know that this was the one woman Adolf Hitler truly loved.

A fleeting romance, and one that ended abruptly when he was forced to return home or face the brutal wrath of a vicious Liverpool gangster he had borrowed money off with no chance of ever paying back.

So when the chance arose of a free berth on a cargo ship back to Austria, courtesy of a Captain, who happened to be an old family friend, then Hitler jumped at it. The worries of a broken heart, so much easily nursed than a broken body.

Suddenly there is movement at the door. He looks over and Admiral Canaris enters. 'My Fuhrer, may I present British Army officer Major James Willard.' Willard approaches Hitler who moves towards him.

He is smiling. 'Major Willard. Welcome to Berlin.'
He offers Willard his hand and the two men shake. Hitler eyes Admiral Canaris, the message clear.
Not needing to be told twice Canaris leaves them alone.
Still no clearer as to what is happening?

'Come sit down with me,' orders Hitler.

He leads Willard over to the fireplace where there are two armchairs.

Willard does so, still clutching tight on the briefcase. Hitler places himself in the opposing chair. His eyes never leaving this Englishman.

'Now I believe you come with a message for me off your Prime Minister, Major Willard?'

'Yes sir.'

'Well it must be extremely important for you to come here personally to deliver it, so I suggest you do so now.'

Willard opens the briefcase and hands over a file to Hitler.

'I have been told to inform you that we have in our custody a young man by the name of Frederick May. We have every reason to believe this is your son sir.'

Hitler is reading through the file. It contains photographs of May. The startling resemblance to the Fuhrer so blatantly obvious it make him shudder.

There can be no doubt.

Willard continues. 'His Mother's name is, I believe you know, Katherine May.' He hands Hitler a photograph of Katherine.

'Unfortunately I'm sorry to inform you Miss May was killed in a car accident a few days back.'

For a moment Hitler appears shell-shocked. His heart breaking at these words.

Finally he looks up at Willard. His voice low, almost whispering. Menacing but measured. 'You say an accident?'

'Yes sir. Miss May was killed along with a policeman. They were returning from Blackpool to Liverpool when it occurred.'

'And what was she doing in Blackpool?'

Willard thinks hard how to phrase the next piece of the story.

'Well sir. I'm afraid to tell you that Frederick May murdered three women in that town in the space of a week. His calling card was to carve a Swastika onto their foreheads. After giving himself up May informed the local police that he would never hang for his crimes because his father would come and save him.'

Hitler listens on intently. Without the words seeming real and somehow out of synch.

Willard stops. 'Are you okay for me to go on sir. There is more. Much more. The reason for me being here indeed.'

'Yes carry on Major' replies Hitler.

'Well after further investigation when the police tracked down Katherine May, she eventually identified you as the father. At this moment in time we have Frederick May imprisoned in the Tower of London as I'm sure you have been made aware of?'

'I received the communique,' replies Hitler.

'Good. Right then' smiles Willard. Though inside his stomach is churning.

'Here is what my Prime Minister proposes.
Mr Churchill will arrange for your son to be brought over here to Germany in exchange for you cancelling your invasion plans and perhaps turning east? Who knows with prevailing winds of war we may in time join you?

The Prime Minister wishes you to know he shares your distrust of Stalin and hatred of Communism. And that no matter how heinous Frederick May's crimes, his place, if you agree to this deal, should be by your side in these troubled times.'

Willard takes a deep breath. 'But if you disregard this plan, he will without mercy and hesitation hang your boy from London Bridge and inform the world of his crimes and who his father is.'

Willard fears the worse as Hitler flashes a look of anger towards him.

But such is the Fuhrer's state of mind his words are lost in a hazy fog.

None of this feels real to him. But he does understand the invasion of Great Britain could well be a monumental and expensive undertaking that could take years to complete. Twice he has offered olive branches and both times Churchill has thrown them back in this face.

But now this makes sense.

Already the idea of operation *Sealion* was appearing less likely every day as Goering's bombers were being obliterated by the RAF's spitfires and hurricanes over the channel and Southern England.

And the boy? How he would like to see him. His actions in murdering the women, obviously trouble Hitler deeply, but somehow in his twisted mind he sees this as a cry for help. So he will agree to Churchill's plan.

'Very well Major. You return to England with my solemn undertaking that Germany will not invade if you deliver my son to me. I will turn east towards Russia, and maybe as you say, we can do business there in the future.

I never meant for this war against England. I gave Churchill every opportunity to stand down and to stay out of my way. But oh no, he had to make speeches and claim he was willing to drown in his own blood.

And I thought then, so be it, and made it my intention he would do such a thing. But now? If he can refrain from opening his drunken fucking mouth every ten minutes and abusing me then maybe this could work.

There was a reason I never chased you back over the channel Major.

You remember that. My natural enemy has always been in the east with those Barbarians in Moscow. It has been your own fault the death and destruction that has rained down upon you. The trouble with the English is you don't like to back down. Never have.

I respect that but ultimately if you cross me it shall be your downfall. I will wipe your so called sceptre Isle off the face of the earth.

Do you understand?'

Willard nods. He has listened on in disbelief.

Quite incredulously Hitler has agreed. He stands facing him.

'Well there really is no time to waste. With your permission I will return to England straight away and inform the Prime Minister of what we have agreed?' Hitler smiles. 'You do that Major Willard.'

They shake hands.

As Willard goes to leave, Hitler calls after him. 'One last thing Major.'

He turns around.

'Yes sir.'

'Katherine May. You swear to me her death was as an accident?'

'I do and it was' replies Willard. 'A tragic accident.'

He knows well that MI6 officer Timothy Mallory had gone too far and much to Winston Churchill's anger had ordered the soldiers to open fire. A war crime undoubtedly and one which when informed horrified the Prime

Minister. Only in such desperate times could this dreadful act be tolerated.

Mallory is amongst their best men and has a free hand. But he was left under no illusion by his Prime Minister when called into 10 Downing Street of his true feelings towards him. Churchill exploding in anger.

'You are not an assassin sir. Not in my name. No more killings or help me God, I will have your neck on a rope.'

But Mallory still thinks he knows best and has decided to act accordingly. For they in time will thank him and his actions in defending the realm will be forgotten and forgiven…And ultimately rewarded.

Again Hitler smiles. 'Such unfortunate timing. But as you claim an accident. Though I will remember you saying this. Go now Major. Tell Churchill that the monster does have a heart.

Like father like son.'

NO BOMBS OR GUNS

Madrid: Model Jail: September 1940: Thirty three Year old Irish Republican, Sean Ryan, is sat chained in a small dark cell. The one tiny window letting in a chink of light is illuminating the dark haired Ryan's heavily bearded face. His green eyes and handsome features engrossed in a tiny, tattered book about the French Revolution in English. Given to him courtesy of a rare show of humanity from a Nationalist prison guard.

Ryan is serving a twenty year sentence for his part in the Spanish civil war, serving as a commanding officer in the International Brigade. Wounded in the Brigade's last major stand at the Battle of the Ebro River, *Batalla del Ebro.*

Ryan was taken prisoner and unlike many of his foreign *compadres,* escaped a firing squad because an eagle eyed Karl Radl, an intelligence officer of the *Abwehr,* remembered him from a surveillance picture taken by an agent in Dublin.

Ryan was once a respected figure in the Provisional IRA hierarchy and Radl arranged for him to be transferred to a prison hospital. In the hope that once recovered, Ryan would show gratitude and help in the expected coming struggle against a common enemy. Great Britain.

However Radl underestimated Ryan's hatred for Fascism, even over the British Empire. The Irishman refused all Nazi offers to co-operate in covert operations against the British and so they left him to rot on Spanish soil. Almost forgotten for two years in his rat infested cell.

Until now.

The grating sound of a bolt being opened on the cell door causes Ryan to look up. Standing there is a prison guard and alongside him fellow Irishman and an old comrade from his days in the IRA. Thirty five year old Liam Russell. Short with dark hair and weary blue eyes. His face telling a tale of Ireland's recent violent history.

Russell is grinning wide. 'So this is where you've been hiding Ryan? You have played a wonderful game of hide and seek. '

Ryan smiles. 'You took your time Liam.'

'Ah it's not as if you were going anywhere is it?'

Russell turns to stare at the guard who immediately leaves the cell. He goes across to Ryan, takes a key from his pocket and starts to unlock the chains.

'What's going on?' Asks Ryan.

Russell smiles and puts his hand on Ryan's arm. 'I've been searching high and low for two years my friend. It was only when I bumped into a former fascist blue shirt in a Dublin pub that was at Ebro. He was drunk and told me a strange story about an Irishman fitting your description. And that you had been brought here.

And now you're leaving this shithole.'

'Where are you planning on taking me?' Asks Ryan

'We are going on a little trip to Berlin to see a little man with a Charlie Chaplin moustache about an interesting proposition.'

Ryan glares at Russell. He holds out both his hands.

'Put the chains back on.'

Russell appears staggered. 'Oh come on Sean man. This is a ticket back home. Besides it's not what you think.'

'These people are fascists Liam. I respect you coming here and I've always valued you a true friend. I would die for you, but I just can't do this.'

Russell shakes his head. 'Listen you pig headed son of Mayo. I'm no great fan of the goose stepping bastards. But when I say by doing this you'll be saving lives. Countless thousands of them, you have to believe me?'

Ryan stares at Russell for a moment. This is a man he trusts.

'Pig headed son of Mayo?'

'Well you're getting on my nerves! And let me tell you something else, I'm not leaving this fucking cell without you Sean Ryan.'

Russell takes one of the chains and puts it on his own hand.

'Now if you want to listen to my moaning and terrible singing for the next eighteen years, then go ahead turn me down.

'What about it then?'

Ryan smiles. 'No guns or bombs?'

'I swear' replies Russell. 'No guns or no bombs. This comes direct from Admiral Canaris. We have done business with him before. You know he can be trusted.'

Ryan offers Russell his hand and they shake.

'Okay' says Ryan.

'Berlin it is.'

The two men embrace.

A Junker transport plane carrying Abwehr intelligence officer Karl Radl and the IRA men Sean Ryan and Liam Russell, lands just outside Berlin, shortly after midnight. As they three men step off the plane they watch as the horizon is lit up red. The RAF have come calling.

'Jesus Christ' exclaims Russell. 'I wouldn't want to be in the middle of that.'

Ryan watches as if transfixed. 'In Prison I was told you were winning this war at a canter Radl.' He points towards the bombing. 'What is this?'

'What is it?' Replies Radl. Clearly irked as his eyes turn towards the thundering skyline. 'Winston fucking Churchill, Irishman.' He declares.

'That's what. The old crow is one defiant bastard.'

Radl motions Ryan and Russell onwards towards a waiting car.

'Come we have business to attend to.'

In a deserted farmyard Admiral Canaris sits and waits at a small table. In front of him a bottle of Schnapps and four glasses. In the distance he can hear the bombs falling on Berlin. Canaris helps himself to a drink and remembers Herman Goering's words to them all at a meeting with the Fuhrer.

The pompous fat oath in his ice cream uniform and racks of ill deserve medals was as ever brown nosing and uttered the immortal quote.

'If the RAF ever drop one bomb on Berlin call me Meyer.'

'Damn you Meyer,' toasts Canaris, as the room illuminates a reddish glow from the far off flames. The Admiral downs the schnapps in one.

The Fuhrer has now informed him of what is occurring and Canaris has moved quick to put a plan in place. Two of the major players are set to arrive shortly.

He has always had a soft spot for the Irish.

Canaris thinks of them as fighting poets. None more than Ryan and Russell. Years before they worked together when the *Abwehr* arranged an arms shipment for the IRA. He found them both perfectly affable and men of honour and their word Also ones not to be crossed. Fine allies in times such as this and above all trustworthy. In present day Berlin with everyone looking to feather their own nest and curt favour with Hitler, men like this are hard to find.

Canaris hears the sound of a car pulling up outside. The banging of doors and suddenly, led by Karl Radl, who offers Canaris a normal army salute, they are entering the farmhouse.

Canaris smiles and walks up to Radl. The two men shake hands.

'It is good to see you Karl.'

'You too Admiral. I'm sure you remember our two friends?'

Ryan and Russell stand behind him. They move forward. Grinning wide Canaris has the look of a father seeing his two sons after many year's absence. 'How can I ever forget. Sean Ryan and Liam Russell.'

He embraces both warmly.

'Come all of you sit down. Let us share some schnapps.'

All four settle at the table as Canaris fills four glasses.

'What shall we drink too?'

'A united Ireland' replies a grim faced Russell.

'Of course' smiles Canaris. 'To a united Ireland and to a victorious conclusion for us all in our battle against the British Empire.'

Ryan eyes Russell rather warily before they all chink glasses and drink.

Okay it is great to see you again Admiral' says Ryan. 'But you do know I've been stuck in a stinking Spanish jail in Madrid for two years?'

Unfortunately Sean that was out of my hands. You can ask your friend here. The SS and Himmler overruled any attempt I made to have you freed.'

Russell nods across to Ryan. 'It's true.'

'Well then' smiles Ryan. Seeing as my good friend Liam here and the wonderful Radl over there will not tell me what this is all about, maybe you could be so kind?'

Again Canaris smiles. He refills their glasses. 'I think we should all have one more drink before I do so.'

Ryan downs the schnapps in one go. Now spit it out Admiral.'

DEAD MEN DON'T TELL TALES

Lieutenant Jan Zumbach has received word from Inspector Sydney Appleton that he desperately needs to see him. The message arrived courtesy of a scribbled piece of paper handed to a Polish soldier on guard duty. And so he sets off to meet the policeman.

An isolated beach spot towards Blackpool's near neighbour Fleetwood, and away from prying eyes on the grassy sand dunes. Zumbach thinks this meeting place strange, but feels Appleton must have good reasons. He makes his way through the dunes, his eyes constantly looking around for the Inspector.

Finally he reaches the wide open sands. The sea is out and the beach deserted. A fierce wind is blowing across the grass, and sand and dust flies into Zumbach's face.

He never sees or hears the three bullets that crash into his chest from the most overgrown area of the dunes.

Lieutenant Jan Zumbach falls dead.

A flock of nearby seagulls suddenly start to shriek loud. A deafening crescendo. A requiem for a fallen murdered soldier far from home. A man appears dressed in army uniform. Captain Timothy Mallory.

He puts his revolver back in its holster. He looks towards the Irish Sea.

'So long my Polish friend. Soon you will be sleeping for eternity with the fish and filth out there. He smiles. 'Better to be safe and sorry don't you think? Dead men don't tell tall tales.'

Unbeknown to Mallory, a lone tramp fast asleep in the dunes was also awoken by the gunshots. He watches hidden. Utterly terrified to even dare breathe. But he will remember forever the killer's face. Especially the scar beneath his right eye.

Inspector Appleton is in his office when the phone rings. He picks it up.
'Hello.'
'Syd its Paddy Owen. We need to talk. Meet me at the normal spot mate?'
With that the phone goes down.
It has just gone ten in the evening at the top of Blackpool tower and Paddy Owen stands alone smoking. He looks out over the town which is in almost total darkness. In the distance he can see a flashing red sky.
German bombers busy again in their efforts to level Liverpool to the ground.
Owen is a worried man. He has news that once more will shake the earth on which his friend Inspector Sydney Appleton walks on.
And then a voice behind him.
'Not thinking of jumping are you old mate?'
Owen turns around and Appleton is stood smiling at him.
'What's going on Pat? '
'I think its best you keep your head down for a while Syd.'
'Why, what's happened?'
'I got a call today from Shamus Bigg. He owns the Seadogs club. I'm sure you know him. A dwarf?'
'Yeah I know him' replies Appleton. 'Horrible little piece of work. What did he have to say?'
'A customer of his. A lowlife tramp called Francis Burns. Bigg does business with him. Burns is a first class pickpocket when he isn't pissed. He was sleeping a

hangover off in the dunes up near Fleetwood. And, well he saw something Syd.'

'Go on.'

'He witnessed a British soldier shooting dead a Polish officer.'

Immediately Appleton feels his blood go cold. He knows. He just knows its Zumbach.

'This Burns, did he get a description of the killer?'

'He said that he had a scar under his right eye. But Burns daren't look too long in case he saw him. Do you think this has anything to do with what you told me?'

'This has everything to do with it Pat. If I'm not mistaken the lad they killed was a friend of mine. He was one of the few who knew of the May's connection with Hitler. And the man with the scar? I know him. He is an assassin working for MI6. Whether he is rogue or carrying out orders, that I don't know. But I have to put an end to this. One way or another I have to make it stop.'

'Syd, I think you should go away for a while. I've a place up in North Wales. A cottage near Anglesey. It's isolated, nobody knows where it is. Go there please. Get out of Blackpool whilst you can.'

'I'm going nowhere old friend. Apart from right now I'm off to see the Polish Commander. A tough bastard called Sosabowski. They will have Lieutenant Zumbach down as missing. Sosabowski deserves to know what's going on. And I'm going to tell him everything, and fuck the consequences.

Screw em all Pat.'

Appleton joins Owen and the two men together gaze out over the black prom. On the far off horizon they watch as Goering's Luftwaffe continues to blitz Liverpool.

'Pat I don't want you involved anymore. None of this is going to end well for anyone.'

Owen smiles. 'You crazy man. You really think I would leave you on your own to face these bastards. Like you say. Screw em all Syd. Me and you against the world. What do you say?'

He offers Appleton a cigarette which he accepts.

'Besides it will be good to play the guy in the white hat for a change.'

Appleton nods in thanks as Owen lights his cigarette.
He inhales.

'There is no good and bad anymore Pat. No black and white either.

Everything is just grey mate.'

Lansdowne Hotel: Polish Headquarters: Inspector Appleton is escorted into a front lounge of the hotel whilst a Polish officer goes to wake General Sosabowski. 'Please wait here Sir.'

Appleton sits down, his mind racing on just how he is going to inform the General that one of his officers has been murdered by British intelligence. Suddenly dressed in pyjamas and dressing gown, General Sosabowski appears. 'Inspector what do you want?'

'General, I have reason to believe Lieutenant Zumbach has been murdered.'

For a second Sosabowski stands stunned. He goes to sit near Appleton.

'Zumbach has been missing since yesterday morning. Are you absolutely certain about this?'

Appleton nods. 'I haven't found his body yet but the information is from a reliable source.'

'A reliable source?' Snaps an angry Sosabowski. 'Who is this reliable source? 'One of my finest officers has been murdered and you speak to me of this. I want you to bring him here now and let me decide on whether he is reliable or not.'

'This man doesn't know who killed Zumbach, General. But I do.'

'Well you best tell me Inspector.'

Ten minutes later Appleton has informed Sosabowski of all that has occurred.

The General sits and listens in a state of shock. He finally stands and goes to open a cabinet. Inside is a bottle of vodka. Sosabowski takes this with two glasses and returns to sit with Appleton. He pours two drinks and passes one over.

'Inspector what you have just told me sounds like the rantings of a madman. But I don't believe you are mad. Zumbach always spoke well of you and Detective Carter. And so I will take what you tell me as the truth. Which means that we and more specifically you and your countrymen have a big problem?'

'What exactly do you mean sir?'

'What I mean Inspector Appleton is I want this bastard's head on a stake, otherwise I promise you I will give the order for my men to wreak hell on this green and pleasant land of yours until we find him. A British agent murdering his own people and allies, just to keep this dirty secret?'

'It all simply defies belief' say Appleton. 'They are obviously working to the notion that dead men don't tell tales.'

'Where is this May?' Asks Sosabowski.

'He was taken to London' replies Appleton.

'God knows what they are planning to do with him.'

'Well I can guarantee Inspector, I intend to find out. Because I possess what you don't. I have push. I have ten thousand poles at my back that have lost a brother in arms. One who fought bravely against the Nazis, only to be butchered here. In a place he had sworn to protect. I will make a phone call to London first thing tomorrow morning. Meanwhile.'

Sosabowski refills both glasses and raises his high.

'To detective Zumbach and Lieutenant Carter.'

Appleton does similar. 'To Katherine May also.'

They toast.

'I was thinking of heading to London myself' says Appleton.

'Try and kick a stink up at the war office. Rattle a few feathers.'

'No you must stay here' insists Sosabowski. 'Why should we go to them? Those sonofabitches can come to us. And not just some measly colonel or some five star general full of remorse and talk of the greater good. No my friend I want to hear this from the man himself.

I want to speak to Winston Churchill.'

IRISH EYES

A car with blacked out windows and a motor cycle escort pulls up outside the Tower of London. It is met by four red capped MPS all carrying sub machine guns. Out steps Major James Willard, Sean Ryan and Liam Russell. An uneasy alliance has been forged between Willard and the two Irishmen. All share one common bond. To deliver Freddie May back into the hands of his blood father, Adolf Hitler, and then wipe their hands of this shocking masquerade. Ryan in particular, though understanding the amount of lives that will be saved by their actions, he remains unsure about the morality of this undertaking. A monster that has murdered three innocent women suddenly becoming a beacon of hope?

The three men step out of the car and MP moves forward to address them. He salutes Major Willard. 'Gentlemen will you follow me please.'

They head inside the tower.

Outside Freddie May's cell two further MP's stand guard. They stand aside as the door is unlocked and Willard, Ryan and Russell enter.

May is sat at a small table. He looks up on seeing his visitors and smiles wide. 'Three wise men. I hope you've come bearing gifts?'

'Listen up May' replies a stone faced Willard.

'You have twenty minutes to prepare for your journey to Berlin. You are to be taken to an airfield in north England. From there you will fly to Ireland, where my two friends here will escort you to a rendezvous with a German U Boat.'

May is smiling wide. 'Who would have believed it? Me and a pair of bomb making Micks. It appears we are on the same side gentlemen.'

Ryan takes a step towards him. One look at his face is enough to wipe the grin off May.

'Firstly I'm a member of the Irish Republican Army. I'm not as you call it a fucking bomb maker. Secondly May, don't make the mistaking of thinking I'm on your side, or that mad bastard of a father of yours in Berlin.

I have no time for the British Empire and I will fight them to the end of my days, but I have even less desire for Fascism, and for low life murdering scum like you. We have got a long journey in front of us. If you want to see Daddy I suggest you keep your mouth shut along the way. Firmly shut. Now do I make myself clear?'

Willard tries hard to not smile at seeing May's cockiness silenced by Ryan's words. Although not knowing them long he has grown to respect and even like his new comrades in arms and does not look forward to the time they once again become enemies.

'So there you have it May' says Willard. 'Anything else to add?'

He shakes his head. Knowing best to stay quiet and not risk a good hiding off the mad Irishman.

Russell walks across so he is only inches from a worried looking May's face.

He is smiling. 'And just for the record Freddie boy, I agree with everything my good friend here has said. Just let me give you some advice my mama gave me many years ago. Sit quiet and don't be heard or by God I will hit you so hard you will arrive in Germany before the fucking submarine.'

May nods. 'I understand'

'Good boy' replies a grinning Russell, who looks over towards Ryan and Willard.' Well boys. I think we should leave Freddie alone for a few moments.' He looks around the dark grimy cell.

'Give him time to gather his thoughts and say goodbye to the rats.'

Somewhere in northern England: The small convoy consisting of four army motorcycles, both front and back of a black Daimler moves fast down a quiet Lancashire country road. The convoy arrives at a seemingly deserted RAF base, consisting only of a landing runway with one transport plane stood waiting and a huge hangar. Two soldiers at the main gates are the only sign of life. They unlock the chains to let them through. Both salute the Daimler as it passes.

The convoy comes to a halt fifty yards outside the hanger. From the front, Major Willard steps out and goes to open the rear door.

Prime Minister Winston Churchill appears. Churchill is smoking a cigar. He eyes the hangar with great disdain.

'Is he in there?'

'Yes Prime Minister. Our Irish friends are already on the plane. They have no wish to spend any more time with May than is necessary.'

'Probably to avoid me also' replies Churchill.

'My actions in Ireland for the crown do not inspire much love for me over in the Emerald isle. Well let's get this over with.'

The two men head over to the hanger. 'Am I doing the right thing here Major?'

'With great respect sir you're the Prime Minister. It's hardly my place to say.'

'You have an opinion don't you?'

'Yes of course.'

Churchill smiles. 'Well I'm damn well ordering you to give it me then?'

'If you insist Prime Minister. The way I see it, there really is no choice. The needs of the many must outweigh the sword of justice for the few. I believe you're doing the right thing sir. Then again I'm a military man. Some people in Blackpool and the victim's families, I'm sure will think different.'

Churchill appears thoughtful. 'Quite. Thank you Major Willard. I'm afraid in these dark and worrying times with the Nazi beast clawing at our door, this frees me from having a guilty conscience. It is the lesser of two great evils.'

They reach the hanger door.

Willard points towards it. 'After you sir.'

They enter this huge dome shaped building. It is empty except for a chained up lone figure, sat on a chair, in the middle of the vast floor. On both sides of him are two Military Police officers armed with sub-machine guns.

The four motor cyclists enter also and surround the Prime Minister. They are carrying small arms.

He looks around. 'Is this really necessary Willard. It's just one man?'

'Sir, if it was up to me I would keep him in a cage until it's time.'

Churchill stares across at the figure on the chair.

'On one man's vile shoulders the future of civilization now lies.'

He takes another long puff on his cigar.

'Come Willard. Let us go tell this creature his fate.'
With their armed escort Churchill and Willard walk
across…

Freddie May smiles. 'So have you come to wave me
goodbye Mr Churchill?
I have to say I'm deeply touched.'
'There are words Mr May, which I would like to use but I
feel to do so would only give you satisfaction. Therefore I
wish only to say that when this war is over, I vow here
now before you to unleash all at my disposal to bring you
back to justice. And that you will pay for the despicable
acts you have committed.'
May has a huge smile on his face.
'You really think you are going to win?'
'It is truly inevitable that good triumphs over evil' replies
Churchill.
'History tells us that in the end men like your father
destroy themselves. A poisonous soul is no match for a
righteous one. A justful cause can be a fearful weapon,
especially when it is backed by brute force. If he dares
comes to these shores then we will use gas on his soldiers
in the water and choke the life out of the invasion. Those
who come from the sky will receive equally no mercy.
They will be bayoneted and shot as they land.
And we ourselves will continue to deliver upon his cities
with our fighter bombers, a firestorm that will make him
curse the day he dared to tug the tail of this island of mine.
Are we understood? The deal?
Your pitiable life for the promise of no invasion?'
May nods. 'I will pass on your comments Mr Churchill.'
He can't help but smile. 'It is good you value me so
highly.'

'I value you lower than the merest sewer rat. let me make that very clear. You are a disease Mr May. One that there is no cure for but the rope.

Always remember that in years to come. For you there will never be peace.'

Churchill looks across to Major Willard, the message clear. The MP's drag May to his feet.

'There is a plane waiting Mr May. It will take you Ireland and from there to Germany. I wish you God speed only in the hope that our deal with Herr Hitler is swiftly realised. In any other circumstances, I would happily pray for you to die a slow lingering death.'

His piece said Churchill goes to leave. Only for May to call after him.

'Could you ever think someone like me would be your salvation Mr Churchill?'

The Prime Minister turns around.

He smiles. 'I am prepared to dance with the devil Mr May, as I believe you surely are. But in the end you and the monster in Berlin will play to my tune. I can promise you that.'…

Once back outside Churchill lights up another cigar. Willard watches him closely. 'I feel unclean Major Willard. Somehow that man has got under my skin.'

'Soon be out of our hair Sir' replies Willard.

Both men stare across at the plane as Freddie May is led in chains up the steps.

Sean Ryan and Liam Russell stand smoking on the tarmac.

'Would you mind sir if I go wish farewell to our IRA friends?'

'You go Major. I will wait in the car. I can feel their Irish eyes glaring from here. Tell them from me I appreciate all their help and won't forget it.'

Willard walks across the runway.

'Here comes the last good Englishman' says Ryan, whilst stamping on his cigarette to put it out.

Russell grins wide. 'Don't you go getting all emotional on us now Major Willard.'

He smiles. 'Good luck gentlemen. Let us hope that if we do meet again it can be in better circumstances. He offers out his hand and both men shake it.

'Same to you' replies Ryan. He points over to Churchill in the car.

'You tell yer man over there to keep his nose out of my country and we'll get on just fine.'

'Take care Major Willard' adds a smiling Russell.

'I agree both with my friend here and your comments. You are not a bad man in spite of the uniform you wear.'

That said Ryan and Russell board the aeroplane. Willard stands well back as the engine roars louder and the propellers pick up power. Slowly it starts to head off down the runway. Then ascending and Ireland bound.

He watches till it is almost out of sight then heads back.

'Thank you sir' says Willard, on stepping into the car.

'We still have much work to do today Major Willard,' replies Churchill.

'Now I must go and see General Sosabowski to try and prevent him declaring a Polish uprising in Blackpool. '

KILLER CLOWNS

Lytham beach: Prime Minister Winston Churchill, General Stanislav Sosabowski and Inspector Sydney Appleton are walking together on a wide-sweeping empty beach. The sea is far out and the three men are surrounded by English and Polish soldiers. Major James Willard is also present, but he keeps a decent distance walking nearby.

Only the sound of seagulls screeching can be heard. The madness of Blackpool sits behind them. Lytham is a haven from the fervid crowds and drunken hysteria that has engulfed the town.

These men have serious business to attend to. Appleton has been invited along by Sosabowski. He believes this English policeman deserves to hear from Churchill's own mouth the reason for such violence committed in his town and against his people.

'First of all gentlemen' begins Churchill. 'May I add my deepest condolences for the deaths of Detective Carter and Lieutenant Zumbach. And also Katherine May. All tragic. This is all such a damned mess.'

Sosabowski stops in his tracks and stares incredulously at Churchill.

'A damned mess? Mr Prime Minister you have both English and Polish blood on your hands. That is so much more than just a damned mess.'

For a moment the prime minister says nothing. He appears hurt by Sosabowksi's cutting remarks. Clearly the fuming Polish General is not set to let Churchill off the hook.

'Let me say straight away to both of you. Captain Mallory was not acting on my orders. His mandate did not include murdering our own. Mallory is out of control and will be dealt with in the most severe of manners.'

'Are you going to hang him?' Asks Sosabowski.

'Like I said General, he will pay for his actions.'

Appleton knows in his heart the Prime Minister will not execute Mallory. For despite the vile murderous acts he remains a vital cog in the war effort. It sickens him and Appleton feels he has to speak up.

'With great respect sir, I don't believe you. Mallory could have been pulled out after Carter and May were killed. He was allowed to stay and the result being he over-stepped the mark once more by gunning down Lieutenant Zumbach. I believe he thinks his actions are justified because of the threat that awaits us across the channel. But in my mind they don't. They simply don't!
Justice must be served. Otherwise what is the difference?'

'Between what Inspector?'

'Ourselves and the Nazis sir.'

'What would you suggest I do then?'

'Leave Mallory to us Prime Minster' Says Sosabowski. 'If as you claim he was acting beyond your jurisdiction then let him pay for his crimes.'

Appleton turns and points back towards Blackpool. The tower as ever prominent over all. 'Mallory has spilled blood on both my town's beaches and streets. Unlike Freddie May, whom you have also shown mercy too, despite butchering three innocent women, this man has to be made accountable for his actions sir.'

Churchill too stares back at Blackpool. He then turns to Sosabowki and Appleton. 'What I have been forced to do with May will scar my soul and haunt me to the day I die. It was done for the greater good. I know you both must find that hard to stomach, but at this moment, as we speak, May is on his way to Germany to be reunited with his father.

It is a *quid pro quo*.

In exchange Herr Hitler will now look east and abandon the invasion.

I have given him false undertaking that in time we may join him as allies against the Soviet Union. I can tell you both now; I will never do such a thing. It was said to give us vital breathing space. For I would rather blow my own brains out than have England fight alongside his Nazi regime.

Oh the war between ourselves and Germany will continue unabated. He will attempt to level our cities and us equally so his. But I played the only card I had gentlemen. It was desperation on my part. For I must admit despite my rhetoric. The speeches of defiance and grim determination to fight them to our last drop of blood. It would have been no contest.

If we couldn't stop them on the beaches, then defeat would have been inevitable. And this island, your town, Inspector Appleton. And your men, General Sosabowski, would have been smashed under the Nazi jackboot.

No amount of courage would have sufficed for we simply do not yet possess the armaments required to fight on. Our guns and tanks sit rusting as everlasting monuments to the disaster that was Dunkirk.

Oh I can admit it to you two here today, but not to anyone else. Not even to myself. I told people only what they needed to hear. For I could not afford to see the British people lose hope.

Hope you see is our last true weapon.

And I can only pray it will be enough to see us through until we are strong again. Now regarding Mallory? So be it. I am now washing my hands of him.

The man is yours to do with what you feel right. Speak to Major Willard over there and he will give you details as to his last known whereabouts.'

'Thank you' says Appleton.

'No thank you Inspector Appleton,' replies Churchill. 'You're a good man sir. And you General Sosabowski. I hope you both find it in your heart to forgive me.'

Sosabowski nods towards the Prime Minister.

He offers his hand and Churchill accepts it. The same with Appleton.

'Now' he continues. 'If you will excuse me, I have a war to win.'…

Sosabowski and Appleton watch the Prime Minister walk off. He stops to whisper into Major Willard's ear.

'Anything they want.'

The Major comes across to them.

'What is it you need?' Asks Willard.

'Arrange a meeting with Mallory' replies Appleton. 'Tell him he's being recalled. No questions asked. Then I'll take care of the rest.'

Willard appears uneasy. 'Very well. But this is not a man to be underestimated. Mallory is extremely dangerous. He is the best of his type we possess.'

Sosabowski smiles. 'The best of his type? Mallory is a murdering sonofabitch Major.'

'Like I said Major Willard,' adds Appleton. 'Tell me when and where and we'll deliver this bastard straight to hell.'

That same night Captain Timothy Mallory stands alone at the top of Blackpool tower waiting for his contact to appear. He is staring out over the rails at the darkened town. It has gone nine o'clock and officially the tower is shut, but a locked door has never been a problem for Mallory.

He has received word that his time on the ground is over.

Mallory is no longer required in the provinces. This man's special talents are needed back in the capital. Spies and fifth columnists abound in London town. The ruthless Mallory knows his methods are thought abhorrent to superiors. None more than Churchill, but he remains steadfast in his mind, all that matters in the end, is to keep this realm safe from Nazi tyranny.

There are no sleepless nights for Captain Timothy Mallory. He is simply following orders and is prepared to ensure nothing or no one ever gets in the way.

'Good evening Captain Mallory.' He turns around and stepping out of the shadows are two men in clown masks aiming revolvers towards him.

Mallory is astonished because the one who spoke is clearly a dwarf. Before he has time to go for his own pistol they open fire and Mallory falls in a hail of bullets.

He lies dying as the hitmen stand over him. Barely alive Mallory tries hard to talk, but can only do so in a tortured, final whisper. 'All I did was for my country.'

That said his eyes close and Mallory passes away.

The men remove their clown masks. It is the owner of *Seadogs*, Shamus Bigg and his boyfriend George Lamb. Bigg leans down to ensure Mallory is definitely dead. 'Right then come on,' he say. 'Let's get this over with.'

Together they pick up Mallory's body and throw him off the tower.

Down he hurls before splattering in a bloodied mess on to the prom. Both stares over the rails at their handiwork. Smiling and satisfied that the job is done.

Bigg wipes his hands together. 'Strange times indeed. The end of days.

Let's go home George.'

The unlikely couple swiftly make their escape…

Reich Chancellery: It is night time in Berlin and amidst a rare lull from the RAF bombing, a car pulls up outside the Chancellery building. It is met by Admiral Canaris and four SS soldiers. From its rear door out steps Freddie May in a German Wehrmacht officer's uniform. A smiling May shakes hands with Canaris and is then swiftly ushered inside.

Through the long-winding red-carpeted corridors of the Chancellery. All bedecked out in Nazi insignia, statues and huge frame portraits of May's father adorning the walls, they walk. Canaris steals a glance at this young man. There can be no doubt of who he claims to be. The similarity is astonishing.

And a little, even for Canaris, a man who has experienced most of what life can throw at you. A little unnerving.

May is throwing Seig Heil salutes around like an excitable little boy feeding bread to the ducks.

He is eyed by all with curiosity and because of the resemblance, sheer fear. May turns to Canaris. 'Are we going to see my father?'

Canaris nods.

May grins wide. 'Everything I did it was for him.'

Canaris' stomach turns. Fully aware this vile monster has killed the three women in Blackpool. 'A family trait' he thinks to himself.

Finally they reach the huge white doors of Hitler's Personal quarters.

It is guarded by two further SS guards, whom both snap to attention at the appearance of Canaris' party.

 They step aside.

 The Admiral turns to Freddie May. 'Your father awaits you.'

Suddenly the smile drains away from May's face. The moment he has dreamed of has arrived and now he dreads it.

 'Is he looking forward to seeing me?'

'Of course' replies Canaris. 'You are the Fuhrer's son. His flesh and blood. Now in you go.'

 He opens the door and May enters.

 Dressed in his finest uniform stands Adolf Hitler. He watches as this figure approaches. This young man. A stranger. His son.

May walks a few steps then appears reluctant. So obviously nervous.

Hitler moves towards him, until only a yard away.

 May smiles. 'Hello Father.'

 Instantly he finds himself embraced. After a lingering moment they come apart.

 'I come with a message from Winston Churchill.'

 Hitler nods. 'Churchill has his deal for now my son. Let us see where the winds of war blow over the next year or so. I may yet make that speech from Buckingham Palace balcony.'

 He puts an arm around May's shoulders.

 'Come, we have so much to discuss.'…

 Inspector Sydney Appleton and Paddy Owen are walking along a busy North pier. It is late September, but the sun is shining. An Indian summer. The crowds are out and the drunken madness shows no signs of prevailing.

A live for today, as tomorrow I may die attitude still exists.

Soldiers, sailors and RAF personnel blowing off steam.

'We dealt with a suicide last night Pat. Tragic. Looks like some poor bastard had too much drink and fell off the tower. The fact he was covered in bullet holes does complicate the matter, but it shouldn't be a problem.'

'Who's working the case?' Asks Owen.

'Me' smiles Appleton.

'Suicide eh' sighs Owen. 'Heard it was a pair of killer clowns myself.'

'Who pulled the trigger?'

'Shamus Biggs and George Lamb?'

'Jesus' exclaims Appleton. 'They are not exactly hard to spot in a line up?'

Owen laughs. 'They are professionals. I promised not to burn their club down if they did this. Besides there will never be a line up?'

'Very True' nods Appleton. 'Good riddance to bad rubbish.'

They reach a multi-coloured booth emblazoned in stars and the words

Madame Marie's. On its wall a poster claims…*Let the Gypsy lady tell your fortune…*

Owen points towards it. 'Maybe we should have just asked her how this was all going to turn out? Save ourselves a whole heap of trouble.'

'Fuckin' crystal ball and magic. All rubbish if you ask me.' Replies Appleton.

Both stop and lean over the rails and look back over the wide expanses of Blackpool's prom.

'This all just feels like one long nightmare Pat.'

'It's far from over yet Syd. Listen, remember that night when I told you and Harry I was saving a special bottle of Scotch whisky for when the Germans arrived? I was going to drink it and then blow the club to kingdom come?'

Appleton smiles. 'Of course I do. How could I forget? The dynamite?'

He smiles. 'We need a chat about that.'

'Well how would you like to share the Scotch with me? We'll toast Harry's memory. And then when it's done I'll open another one.'

'Sounds good. I miss him. He was like a son to me. So much blood Pat. Wasted lives.'

This is a war old mate. People die. Not many of our young ones today will be allowed the privilege of old age.'

Owen puts an arm around Appleton's shoulders.

'Maybe this is not a story to tell our Grandchildren, but one thing is certain we can always claim.'

'What's that?' Asks Appleton.

Owen smiles. 'That once upon a time in Blackpool we did the right thing.'...

EPILOGUE

Blackpool today: The old man, Freddie May moves away from the window and sits back upon his bed. On the cabinet is a tiny tin box. He opens it up. Inside is a crumpled old black and white photograph. It is of him alongside his father. Both men are smiling.

Back then everything went swiftly wrong for May in Berlin.

Once his true nature shown itself and lack of any notable qualities became obvious, Hitler moved fast to wash his hands of this 'blood' son. Fatherly love disappeared overnight when May raped a housemaid at Berchtesgaden. *'The Eagle's nest.'* The Fuhrer's Bavarian mountain castle-fortress.

Admiral Canaris was instructed to inform May he had to leave. Hitler could never bring himself to execute his own flesh and blood and so instead he placed one million American dollars in an Argentine bank.

A plan was put in place for May to travel to Buenos Aires and make contact with an *Abwehr* officer. A message from Hitler was whispered into May's ear. Passed on by the German agent on his arrival. It was simply ever tell anyone who you are and we will find and kill you.

And so for seven decades May lived anonymously in South America.

Only returning home in his later years. Certain the murders of the three women and his notorious blood line would be long forgotten. Buried and lost in the annals of time.

He was right.

And so Freddie May now lies down on the bed. He clutches tight the photograph and closes his eyes for the last time. This dreadful tale finally dying with him.

Outside Blackpool parties on...

.

The End

Made in the USA
Monee, IL
11 June 2021

71038760R00075